DECEPTION
MAFIA DADDIES BOOK 3

BJ ALPHA

Copyright © 2024 by B J Alpha

All rights reserved.

No part of this book may be reproduced in any form or by any electronic or mechanical means, including information storage and retrieval systems, without written permission from the author, except for the use of brief quotations in a book review.

This book is a work of fiction. Characters, names, places and incidents are products of the authors imagination or used fictitiously.

Any similarity to actual events, locations or persons living or dead is purely coincidental.

Without in any way limiting the author's exclusive rights under copyright, any use of this publication to "train" generative artificial intelligence (AI) technologies to generate text is expressly prohibited. The author reserves all rights to license uses of this work for generative AI training and development of machine learning language models. No audio files can be produced without the authors written consent beforehand.

Published by: Alpha Team Publishing.

Edited by: Dee Houpt.

Proofread by: Mackenzie of Nice Girl, Naughty Edits.

Cover Design: Katie Evans.

Dedication

For every girl who longs for a better life.
    A better man.
    There's someone out there waiting for you.
    He might just be waiting for the perfect time to make his move.

BLURB

Rocco

The moment I set my eyes on her I wanted her.

I had to play the long game for her to be in the perfect position for the taking.

I've lied and manipulated to create the textbook moment for me to make my move.

So, when I walk into her classroom as her new student, I have everything in place.

I'm coming for you, Little Red.

And nothing you say will stop me.

NOTE FROM AUTHOR

This book contains sensitive subject matters, tropes and content that some readers may find unsuitable.
Please see my website for full details.

Prologue

Rocco

The blonde pressing kisses down my neck makes my skin itch. Of course she knows how old I am—they all do—yet they still fawn over me like they do the rest of the men in my family. The desperate, hungry whores leave me with little to no satisfaction. What I need is something different; I just don't know how to find it.

My father winks in my direction, and that pisses me off further. I'm nothing like him, nor do I want to be. He thinks having a woman as his plaything to use as he sees fit and dispose of as if they're nothing is the only way to have a relationship with the opposite sex. Something inside me craves more. When I have sex, it's a means to an end. Sure, I enjoy it at the time, but I'm never truly fulfilled. I'm missing the connection, and I'm well aware I won't ever get it with any of the whores my father parades around.

Getting my cock hard can be a chore, and I grimace every time a woman attempts it. I've often wondered if I'm broken, if the incidents I witnessed growing up have caused some inner trauma, or if I'm just bored with the mundane scenes that play out around me. Maybe I'm so used to them and they're so freely available that they simply don't hold the appeal they should.

They never really have.

When the blonde places her hand over my zipper, I fight the urge to lash out. My skin feels like it's crawling with insects at her touch. Instead of throwing her to the floor and drawing my knife to punish her like I want to, I push off the couch, away from her and her grabby hands, and stride toward the balcony overlooking the dance floor of my father's club Sinners.

The strobe lights flicker around us, and the bass of the music makes the floor vibrate beneath my feet as I take another pull of my beer. I may only be sixteen years old, but I've been drinking, fucking, and committing crimes in the name of La Familia since I became a made man at thirteen.

Music plays out like background noise, along with the high-pitched squealing of the topless girls my father throws money at. I shake my head as anger courses through my veins. Surely there's more to life than this?

I down the rest of my beer, then place the empty bottle on the nearest table and stare down at the sea of people dancing. Each one of them having an amazing time in the throes of their happiness. With every move, they're letting go of their troubles, allowing the music to provide them with an outlet for their tensions and freeing their minds—a luxury I'll never be allowed.

My eyes survey the crowd, and as if on instinct, I note our security detail littered among the guests, hidden in plain sight. When I follow the line of guests standing at the bar, my gaze lands on a face that holds my breath hostage and causes my mouth to go dry. As I take her in, my heart stutters. Her thick, wavy red hair brightens her pale skin as the lights flicker over her. The red dress she wears fits her like a glove, emphasizing her curvy physique, causing my cock to appreciate her hour-glass figure and beauty like never before.

My gaze trails from her red high heels, over her exposed legs, and up toward her shapely hips. Something I've never encountered with the women my father parades around us, yet I'm grateful. This woman needs shielded from all others; she is mine. I quickly glance over my shoulder, checking to see that nobody else is staring at or lusting after her, then I snap my eyes back down to her, desperate to keep her in sight for as long as possible.

She's short, even in the heels she wears, and I lick my lips at the fullness of her tits. As my curiosity piques, I find myself leaning over the balcony to see if I can make out a bra holding them in place or not. Annoyance rumbles through me when I realize I'm too far away, but something tells me those generous tits of hers are real too. They seem to fit her figure perfectly. My mouth waters to taste them, to savor the weight in my palms, to caress them and toy with her nipples tenderly while embracing her fullness and basking in her attributes. A need consumes my bloodstream, so full of determination that nothing will stop me from having her, and I smile at the prospect.

Little Red is mine.

When someone approaches her, my hands grip the balcony railing, and the way she steps back out of his reach has anger surging through my veins at an alarming speed. She doesn't like the man, and that thought alone puts a mark on his head.

My jaw aches from clenching so hard I'm surprised my molars don't shatter.

"Roc, Gerrard Davis, the police commissioner's son, and his wife would like to wish you a happy birthday in person," Silas, my right-hand man, speaks in my ear. He's been at my side since I was thirteen years old, and while I've always welcomed his presence, right now I want nothing more than to tell him to fuck off.

My eyes never leave the woman, and I hate the fact I can't hear what they're saying, but it's clear they know one another when his hand finds her hip and he draws her closer to him. Jealousy unleashes inside me and venom floods my veins.

She attempts to shrug him off, and his grip tightens, causing a red haze to cloud my vision as I contemplate all the damage I will unleash on his body, starting with his hand.

Silas clears his throat. "Roc?" His tone is firmer this time.

DECEPTION

"Tell him I'm busy getting my cock sucked," I state without giving him my attention, and he chuckles before turning and walking away, leaving me to be consumed by my little red.

As the man brushes hair from her face, my knuckles whiten from the grip I have on the railing. Every cell in my body wants to annihilate him, torture him slowly for daring to touch what belongs to me.

Silas works through the crowd, pulling my attention from them. *Why is he going over to her?* He pulls the guy by the arm, and when Gerrard Davis's face comes into view, Silas's words sink in as he bends to deliver my reply in Gerrard's ear.

Fire burns my blood as my palms become painful against the metal, and the realization of who she is sends a tsunami of fury through me.

My little red is his wife.

Her gaze shoots over Gerrard's shoulder, and her eyes unwittingly land on me. She can't see me; we have privacy glass up here for a reason. Yet, as she stares in my direction, I swear she's piercing my soul, and a strange sense of calmness washes over me. Unlike moments ago, when jealousy and anger flashed through me at an alarming pace.

Gerrard turns from Silas to speak to her, but her gaze never wavers.

That's right, Little Red, give me your attention.

It's like the glass doesn't exist between us, and as my heart hammers with a newfound exhilaration, I know our story is only beginning.

It will cause one hell of a war, but it'll be worth it.

"Happy birthday, son." My father's firm hand clamps over my shoulder as he gives it a sharp squeeze.

"Thank you," I state, my gaze still on her, and the way her eyes scan the screen as if searching for something sends a rush of excitement through me. She's seeking me, I can feel it in my soul. She just doesn't realize it yet. But she will soon enough.

"I have some girls waiting for you." His tone is full of glee, and if I wasn't so transfixed, I'd roll my eyes.

When I force myself to turn to face him, I feel the loss of her instantly. "Not tonight. I have plans."

His lips curl up at the side.

Whatever he thinks he knows, he doesn't. Nobody does.

Not even me.

All I know is, my obsession with Little Red has been triggered, and nothing will stop me from taking her.

Not my father.

Not the Mafia.

Certainly not her husband.

I'm coming, Little Red, and when I catch you, I'm never letting you go.

Chapter One

Hallie

Two years later ...

"Can you believe we got VIP passes? Like, how the hell did you win the competition again?" Sharna's eyes light up as she tops up the cocktail glasses so much it sloshes over the rim with her excitable giggle. My friend has been an incredibly supportive over the years, especially lately. She even moved back to New Jersey to carry me through my divorce and help me find the perfect rental. Nights I didn't want to be alone, she stayed with me, and now she only lives a ten-minute drive away. So, she was the obvious person to bring as a plus one for a giveaway I won that I didn't even know I'd entered.

"I'm really not sure. I know Gerrard came here a few

times; we came together a couple of years ago." I take another sip of the fruity cocktail I've already forgotten the name of. "Maybe he entered the giveaway and gave them my email at some point." I shrug.

She scrunches her nose at the mention of Gerrard, and who can blame her? My friend is protective of me, and I love her for it. We grew up more like sisters than anything else, and our bond is unbreakable.

"Mm, the douche probably thought he was being clever spamming your inbox with junk mail," she states before taking another drink.

I'm really not sure Gerrard would think of signing me up for spam emails, but if he did, I'm kind of glad. A night out is just what we needed.

"So, how are the wedding plans coming along?" I ask, and her lips purse.

"Honestly?" She quirks an eyebrow at me, and I nod for her to continue. "I don't like all the photos of the quaint little chapels you send me, Hal. I want big, elaborate." She throws her arm out for emphasis, and I grimace. I had an elaborate wedding with Gerrard and hated every second of it.

"Okay, well, what about instead of a chapel, you could hire a venue and have the wedding and reception there?"

"Like where?"

I take another sip of my drink and tap my lip while my mind races with all the suggestions Gerrard's family had for our wedding. "A ballroom in a well-known hotel? A manor home? A golf club? A marquee?" I suggest.

DECEPTION

"I'll let the wedding organizers look into it." She waves her hand at me, and I laugh. Sharna never likes to do the work herself, hence why she asked me. "I just thought with you having experience you'd have some good ideas." I ignore her words. The cute little chapel I sent her was my good idea.

"Oh, shit. Don't look now. Hot dude alert." Her eyes widen, then she dips her head as she speaks, and her blonde locks curtain her face. She takes another drink, making me giggle at her schoolgirl antics.

I lift my head and lock eyes with the most intense stare I've ever come across. It has my blood pumping rapidly and my heart rate escalating. This man is hot as the Sahara Desert, causing my mouth to become just as dry.

He swaggers toward us, and his gaze holds a familiarity I can't fathom. It's like I know him, but I don't recognize him. His jeans fit him perfectly, his white T-shirt is stretched over his chest so cinched you can make out his pecs, and he's wearing a leather jacket.

A leather jacket, for Christ's sake.

Gerrard only ever wore a suit jacket and khaki pants. I grimace at the way my mind went immediately to him, but he's the only comparison I have.

The guy's hair is messy but somehow styled. How the hell is that possible? I itch to push my fingers through it and sniff his neck as I do. *To climb ... Jesus, Hallie, you need to get laid.*

Oh, dear god, I need some therapy; this is not normal. *Be normal, Hallie.*

"Can I sit down?" He points toward the chair beside me, but I can't seem to construct words, so Sharna nudges my hand and side-eyes me.

Get a grip, Hallie.

I clear my throat and smile tightly. "Sure."

Jesus, when the hell did I become so damn awkward? I shove the thought of Gerrard's taunts to the back of my mind as he settles beside me. His leg brushing mine sends a blazing heat through my body as his warmth creeps through my skin.

Holy shit, I'm like a love-struck teenager who doesn't know how to function.

"What's your name?" he asks, and his smooth, confident baritone voice does something to me that renders me speechless.

"I'm Sharna." Sharna holds her hand out toward the guy, and he stares at it. Something inside me doesn't want him touching her, but that's ludicrous.

His hand slides into hers, and he gives it a quick shake, then moves it beneath the table and wipes his palm on his jeans. Sharna didn't witness the action, as her dreamy smile remains plastered on her pretty face, and I snort at how obvious she's swooning right now.

"You never said your name?" he whispers into my ear as he places his arm over the back of my chair. When his hand brushes my neck, my brain misfires. "I guess I will just call you my little red, huh?"

I roll my lips while contemplating his nickname for me. Those gray eyes of his bore into mine like he's desperate for a taste of me, and the thought has excitement humming through my body, begging for his touch.

A shudder runs through me, and he pulls back, gifting me with a smirk, as if knowing my body's response to him.

I straighten my shoulders. "Hallie. My name's Hallie."

Lips quirking at the side, his gray eyes flicker over my face. "Nice to meet you, Hallie." His smooth voice caresses my heart, and his sandalwood cologne permeates the air, making me want to sniff him wantonly. I become wet at his proximity, and his commanding aura turns me to putty in his strong hands. It's like his presence demands my attention, and my body willingly obeys.

"Rocco."

Heat creeps up my neck and over my cheeks as the room becomes thick with an indescribable haze.

His tongue darts out over his top lip, and I swear I almost combust.

Jeez, why is everything about him so hot.

"I think little red suits her." Sharna cuts in, breaking the sexual tension bubbling between us.

He takes a drink of his beer, and his eyes devour me while I try to suppress the whimper lodged in my throat. Then he places the bottle back on the table and turns toward me. With his hand over the back of my chair, he toys with my hair, and I find the action hypnotic. "You're not married, Little Red." He nods toward my finger, and I register it as a statement, not a question. "Do you have a boyfriend?"

I open my mouth to speak.

"No, she doesn't. She's totally available. Completely single," Sharna says, and I swear I could slide beneath the table at the eagerness of her words. Heat deepens the red on my cheeks as embarrassment sets in.

He laughs. "Does she always answer for you?" The amusement in his eyes has me smiling back at him, and I open my mouth again to respond.

Sharna leans forward to speak. "Only when needed. And right now, she needs a guy to show her a good time." His eyes never leave mine, as if I'm the only woman in the room. I choke on thin air, and Rocco chuckles, so his muscles pull his T-shirt tighter, and I itch to explore them.

His lips part, but his words are cut off by a shrill ringtone coming from his jacket, and his jaw clenches. "Excuse me a minute." He nods toward us both, then stands and pulls his phone out as he walks away with a confident swagger toward the balcony, and I'm unable to take my eyes off him.

Even his ass is hot.

"Holy fucking shit balls with bells on. He is finnne!" Sharna leans across the table, breaking my train of thought and bringing my gaze back to her. "He wants to fuck your brains out, Hal." She wiggles her eyebrows.

My eyes widen on her words. "What? No. No, he doesn't." I shake my head.

"Yes. Yes, he does." She nods frantically. "And you're going to let him." Pouring another drink from the jug, she pushes it toward me.

DECEPTION

Panic crawls up my spine. "No. I can't." I haven't been with anyone since Gerrard, and he's literally the only person I've been with.

"Yes. You are. You need to get back in the saddle and ride that hot specimen until he breaks, or breaks you, whichever comes first." She shrugs like her words are no big deal.

I snort at her words, then glance over her shoulder toward the hot specimen.

"I don't know him." I chew on my lip. Could I really do this? Have sex with a total stranger?

"Perfect. He doesn't know you or that douche you were married to." She's right, he doesn't know me or Gerrard; he doesn't know the burdens I hold. It's simply one night of fun. That's all.

One night.

"I haven't had sex in so long, Sharn," I say as I stare down at the table.

"Better, still. It'll be like he's breaking you in all over again." I shoot my eyes up toward hers, and her eyebrows dance. "The right way," she tacks on, with a dig at Gerrard's lack of skills.

I take him in once again. "He kind of looks young?"

"Perfect. No dad bod." She nods enthusiastically with a wave of her hand.

"Gerrard doesn't have a dad bod."

"He didn't have skills either. That guy"—she throws her thumb over her shoulder—"will know how to make you scream."

My eyes trail over him. Jeez, he's hot, in a bad boy

kind of way, which is the complete opposite of my perfectly put together ex. On the surface, at least.

Tattoos cover his hands and sneak out of his T-shirt up his neck, and I lick my lips at the thought of exploring them.

Gerrard doesn't have tattoos. He's always been so clean-cut, but this guy, this guy is different, and my body seems to like it.

"He's young," I whisper again, as if trying to talk myself out of it.

If I was guessing, I'd say early twenties, and when I'm thirty-three, that feels like a huge jump. Too much.

"Hell yes, he is!" Sharna practically screams while I wince at her overenthusiastic reaction. Then she lowers her tone. "He will be eager to please you. A young stallion for you to ride. Plenty of stamina. Sounds perfect to me." Her eyes become dreamy, then they reach mine and soften. "Hal, you deserve some fun. It'll give you a confidence boost. Go for it!" I contemplate her words. She knows I've only had sex with Gerrard, and I've been struggling to get into the dating scene despite numerous proposals. "Look, all you need to do is fuck him. Nobody is saying it's for more than one night." She pours more cocktail into my glass with an excitable grin, and a smile tugs at my lips. She's right, a night I can do.

As I move to pick up the glass, a shadow looms over us, and I lift my head to face Rocco. His eyes bore down on me and darken as I wither beneath his stare and swallow at the intensity behind it. There's something possessive lying within it, and a slither of unease ripples through me before I push it to one side. "I think she's trying to get me drunk." I glance toward the cocktail in my hand and feign a chuckle.

"Doesn't matter to me. I'm happy to take you either way, but not going to lie ..." He leans down, only inches from my face, and our eyes are magnetized. The atmosphere becomes electric as he brushes a lock of hair from my face and pushes it behind my ear. "I prefer you to be conscious the first time I take you." Smirking, he pulls back, and I feel his loss instantly. The way his aura controls my body without physically trying feels like something profound, like I'm discovering a part of me I never knew existed, and more importantly, I'm willing to submit to it.

My mind tries to play catch-up with what he just did and said, but it whirls with the latter, as if I'm subconsciously pushing everything else from my brain like a well-oiled machine.

"First time?"

He licks his lips like a predator, and I squirm, never feeling so vulnerable yet so alive. His eyes bore into mine like he's devouring my soul.

His intentions toward me are clear as hunger rolls off him in aggressive waves.

"She's good to go." My head snaps toward Sharna, but I don't have time to react to her words before she's thrusting my purse into my chest and nodding toward the guy. My mouth falls open at her forceful actions.

Not giving me time to second-guess, Rocco holds his hand out toward me, and when I slip mine into his, static electricity flashes through me. His touch takes my breath away, and when he shudders, I know he felt the same energy. It's like a fire has started burning and someone threw gasoline on it, igniting me with a feeling of determination like no other; I need him, if only for tonight.

I need to feel free.

Chapter Two

Rocco

Holding her against my chest, I breathe her familiar, intoxicating scent into my bloodstream while running my free hand over her back and into her hair, then I jerk her head back.

"I hope you're ready for me, Little Red," I growl, and her pupils dilate perfectly.

Having her in my arms has my legs feeling like lead. Every move I made over the past two years has prepared me for this moment. Everything is slipping into place with her in my arms, where she was always meant to be.

I bided my time, diligently waiting for the perfect time to strike, and what better way than to celebrate my coming of age with the perfect gift to myself.

Her.

Of course, I will keep that little nugget of information to myself for now. My little red is vulnerable and needs reassurance, and I intend to give her all the comfort she requires while she serves me so beautifully.

My arm remains wrapped around her like a coiled viper as I guide us through the crowd toward a back entrance. My security nods as we step past them and head down a concealed corridor obstructed by a speaker.

"Where are we going?" she whispers as she lifts her head, her eyes searching mine for an answer.

"My lair, Little Red." My lips twitch at the way she swallows. Then she giggles as if I was joking, and every coiled muscle in my body unfurls at the beauty of its innocence.

I press the elevator button and bury my head in her hair, nuzzling her like an animal coating his body in the scent of his mate.

When we step into the elevator, a shiver runs down her spine. I find her eyes in the mirrored walls, and our gazes remain frozen. She's scared but excited, nervous yet filled with desire. I lick my lips like she's my prey, and she chews on her bottom lip as if sensing my thoughts, and the prospect of devouring her has my cock twitching.

When the elevator moves, I flick my eyes over us in the mirror. Tucked beneath my arm, she's huddled against my chest with her small hand resting on my pec. She's small but fiery, delicate yet strong, and her curves are my undoing. As I glide my gaze over the swell of her tits pushed against me, my cock leaks, and for the first time tonight, I worry I'm going to disappoint her. Her eyes narrow, as if reading my thoughts.

My fingers twitch, so I give in and run them through

DECEPTION

her red hair. "Fuck, Little Red. Daddy's going to have so much fun with you."

She gasps, and I want nothing more than to shove my tongue between her parted lips, giving her no choice but to accept me and my warped words.

The elevator stops, startling her, and my body cramps at the thought of her distress and nervousness. "Don't worry, I got you, Little Red," I whisper in a foreign gentle tone against her curls.

I guide us through the apartment and into my bedroom, and when she steps away from me, I feel it in my core, but I allow her the distance as she studies my room despite me wanting to force her touch on me.

My eyes never leave her as I pick up the champagne sitting on my dresser for the special occasion and pop the cork. The bubbles spill over as I pour us each a glass, and she turns to face me. Little does she know the significance behind today.

My birthday.

"Were you expecting company?" She lifts an eyebrow.

"Only you, Little Red." I stare back at her with truth in my eyes.

She scoffs and giggles. "Right."

I step toward her, carrying the glasses in one hand, then bend down to lift her chin with my fingers. "I'd never lie to you."

Her eyes ping-pong over my face, as if searching for the truth behind my words.

"Okay," she breathes out, and her shoulders relax.

Her trust and compliance mean everything to me, and my chest swells with pride.

I give her a satisfied nod, then swallow down my drink, shrug off my jacket, and throw it on the chair before toeing off my combat boots and socks. Then I sit on the edge of the bed. She plays with the stem of her glass, and I can't help but think how adorable she is as she averts her gaze from me. I'm going to have to make a move before she backs out. I snap my hand out and tug her by the hem of her skimpy black dress until she stands between my legs. One of her hands finds my shoulder while the other clings onto her glass for dear life.

"Finish your drink, baby," I whisper, and love the chill that breaks out across her body as I speak.

She does as I ask, so beautifully submissive, yet so unaware, then I take her glass from her and place it on the carpet.

Her gaze meets mine, and heat creeps over her cheeks as she stares into my eyes. So fucking innocent. "What now?" she whispers.

"Now, take off your dress like a good girl." Her breath hitches, pupils dilating, and I smirk. She's perfect.

Her hand shakes as she pushes the fabric over the swell of her heavy tits toward the flare of her hips, where she wiggles it down until it pools at her feet.

My lungs seize; I've waited a long time for this moment, so fucking long the enormity of it makes it difficult for me to breathe. A pang of urgency to make this as memorable as possible hits me in my heart. This is it, this is our time. The moment I make her mine.

DECEPTION

Her hazel eyes sparkle with uncertainty, and I want nothing more than to banish it away forever.

"You're beautiful," I choke out in awe, meaning every damn word of it. Her pale skin is creamier up close, perfect for me to mark her with an eternal display of our love for one another.

Her flush deepens, spreading over her chest, and I grab a hold of her hips and hoist her up so she straddles my lap, and her skin against mine is like liquid fire. Our lips clash as I take a hold of her ass and clamber up the bed until my head reaches the pillow. My tongue fights against hers as I hold her jaw in my palm before she gives in to my control and allows me to consume her as she does me.

She bucks when I squeeze her ass cheek roughly, and when she grinds over my solid cock, a foreign sound of satisfaction rumbles in my chest. Then she pulls back, breathless, and I swear everything about her is incredible: the smattering of freckles on her chest, her perfectly plump bow lips, the prettiest shade of green specks in her familiar hazel eyes, and the way her tits heave as she breathes has my grip on her tightening.

"Can you lose your T-shirt?" she pants out.

I nod frantically and sit up, tugging it from my back and over my head, then I drop it to the floor.

"Holy hell, you're divine."

I laugh, then a pained sound leaves my chest as her hands splay over my tattooed abs. Her touch sears me with her brand, scorching me for keeps.

"You're hot as hell," she mumbles, completely

unaware of the effect she has on me. Knowing how attracted to me she is has me puffing out my chest and thrusting my hips.

Her eyes widen as her hands trail up my chest until they reach my throat, then she cups my jaw and leans forward, and when she lowers her face to mine, she steals my ability to function. Fabric drops between us, and my mind scrambles to figure out what just happened, but her soft lips rest over mine, and it's quickly forgotten until her nipples brush over my chest and my balls draw up.

"Shit, I need to be inside you," I growl.

She smiles against my lips as her tongue seeks entrance into my mouth, and I willingly accept it. I'll always accept anything she's prepared to give me.

As our tongues tangle, I struggle beneath her to unbuckle my jeans and release my painful cock. "I really need to be inside you." My eyes roll as she tugs on the strands of my hair while grinding her perfect little panty-covered pussy over the tip of my raging cock.

"Mmm," she mewls into my mouth as if lost in our passion, and as my pent-up orgasm builds, I give her no choice and slip her panties to the side. My eyes roll at the warmth of her wetness while I press the head of my cock to her slick hole. Then I lift her ass with the next grind of her hips and slam her down on top of me.

Her mouth falls open as her nails pinch into my shoulders. "Oh god."

I push up inside her, relishing the stretch of her pussy as she wiggles to accommodate me.

"Fuck," I mutter as I hit her cervix.

DECEPTION

"Play with your tits. Feed me your fucking nipple, Little Red." The words fall from my mouth in desperation. I want it all. Need it all.

"Oh god," she pants, and pushes her tits together as I place kisses all over the softness of her, and her pussy clenches with each touch.

The feeling of her encompassing me is phenomenal. After waiting so long to finally feel her, a climax of emotions unleashes as I savagely fuck up into her, giving her no choice but to release her tits and hold on to my shoulders.

My eyes dart between her face and her heavy tits bouncing and swaying. She clings to me for support, no doubt leaving fingernail marks I would happily beg for. "That's it, ride that thick cock, Little Red."

Her eyes flash with lust, and her lips part on my words, and I know then and there that my girl loves a filthy mouth, and I have it in abundance for her.

"Daddy's stretching your little cunt for his thick cock, Little Red."

Her pussy clenches around me.

"Be a good fucking girl and take all Daddy has to give you." I pinch her clit, and she throws her head back. Then I wrap my hand around her throat, surging deep inside her while I use the other to slap her ass hard, determined to take everything I've dreamed of in this moment and leave my mark on her as she will on me. I slap her ass harder, and my eyes roll when she tightens around me.

"Rocco, I'm ..." Her pussy grips me like a vise as her

orgasm hits her so strongly, her body becomes rigid almost instantly.

After waiting so long to have her, I can't hold back any longer. "Fucking take Daddy's cum in your cunt, Little Red." I erupt, coating her insides with my pleasure. Slowly, I release my hold on her as she falls forward against my chest, bringing our perfectly in sync hearts together. They beat erratically while I wrap my arms around her and nuzzle into her hair, embracing this moment before our lives change forever.

I might be about to disappoint my father for the first time in my life, but I will also make him proud. With Hallie by my side, I will gladly give La Familia my everything.

I just need to ensure I have her first.

Hallie

I've never come so hard in my life. The way Rocco looks at me like I'm his everything is all-consuming and renders me speechless. His gaze devours me as if absorbing every inch of me, and the way his body vibrates beneath my touch makes me feel powerful, like I own a part of him that needs me so desperately it eats away at him.

The undercurrent that ran between us became catalytic. An explosion of senses when we finally collided, leaving me draping over his chest. He nuzzles into my hair and breathes in, almost as if memorizing me, and even that thought brings me warmth. I made a man so intoxicated with me he's become feral, giving me confidence I've never felt until today, especially when my ex left me feeling so beneath him and unworthy.

"Fuck, that didn't last as long as I hoped for." He chuckles. "Don't worry, I have plenty of stamina to keep me going." I smile into his chest, then squeal when he flips me over and tears my panties from me. His thick cock is still hard, and I hadn't realized that was a possibility until now.

He thrusts his hips forward, making my tits jiggle, and his eyes peruse my body, from my face down to where we're connected. "Fuck, look at us, Little Red. You're so full of me."

I bite into my lip and lean up on my elbows to stare down. Seeing him rooted so deep inside me has all my inhibitions flying out the window as my pussy clenches around him.

"You like that, huh, my cock deep inside you?" As he rolls his hips, I fall back onto the pillow, and he lifts my arms above my head, holding my wrists together at the headboard. He pulls his cock almost all the way out, then slams inside me so forcefully I wince at the bite of pain coming from his thickness hitting my womb.

"Jesus." I whimper.

His lips tip up into a smirk. "I can feel my cum trickling out of your pussy." He slams inside me again. "It feels so damn good knowing I can come in you."

My body stills, and he chuckles. "Don't worry, Little Red. I'm clean. My cock has been waiting for you." I nod, drunk on his control. His pace picks up, and all I can do is lift my hips in time, meeting him thrust for thrust as arousal zips through me.

"Rocco. Feels. So. Good," I cry out between each slam of his wonderfully powerful hips. The tattoo-covered muscles contract with each thrust, and I make a mental snapshot of the vision before me.

Hotness personified.

DECEPTION

"Fuck, yes." He grinds his hips. "Scream for me, Little Red. Scream for Daddy to fill you." Using the word daddy is so hot and forbidden that my pussy is contracting around him. His warm cum drips from me, and all I can think about is him gifting me with more. His hips slam against me harder this time, grinding against my throbbing clit, and I explode around him. White lights dance before my eyes as my screams of pleasure fill the room.

"Daddy, please ..."

"Holy. Fuck," he says through gritted teeth as his pace stutters and his cock expands deep inside me, sending me further over the edge than ever before. My vision blurs, and he continues to move above me. Sweat coats his forehead, and I itch to push back his hair, to witness the ferocity of his face as euphoria overtakes him, but I'm powerless, simply a broken sail for his ship as we float into the abyss.

His warmth continues to fill me as he draws out his orgasm with short snaps of his hips, then he falls beside me and tugs me onto his chest. His heart races beneath me, and I melt into his tenderness. "Fuck, so damn good, Little Red." The reverence in his words sends a shock wave of confidence through me. My hand trails over the abundance of tattoos covering his abs, and I decide I want to go further and leave a mark on him as much as he is on me.

This night will be ingrained in my mind forever, and I intend to make sure he never forgets his little red.

I place kisses over his chest, delighting in the way his

heartbeat kicks against my lips, then I slink down his body.

"Fuckkk," he pants as he lifts his hips, thrusting his wet cock toward me. "Are you going to taste yourself on me?" His filthy words send a flash of desire through me, and I become drunk on his lust, determined to show him as much passion as he's shown me.

"I'm going to lick my daddy's cock clean." I smile, and a thrill zips up my spine at how his eyes become hooded. The choked noise coming from his throat has me rubbing my wet thighs together.

"Yeah?" he pants.

I nod against the perfect V leading to the smattering of closely trimmed hair surrounding his cock, then dart my tongue out to follow the route. "Then I'm going to suck all around here." My hand finds his sack, and I squeeze it, causing his lips to part and a breathy moan to escape him. "And I'm going to lick up here." My hand travels up his silky length. "And clean here for you." I swipe my thumb over his swollen head, and he flinches.

"Fuck, Little Red. If you keep tormenting me, I'm going to face-fuck you so goddamn hard it's going to hurt." His teeth grind, and I grin.

"Mmm." I lick up his length and swirl my tongue around the head, tasting myself on the tip. A shudder racks through him while I pump him faster on each upstroke, and his fists coil into the sheets, allowing me the time to explore.

"Fuck. Wrap those lips around me, Little Red." He lifts his hips. "Lick Daddy's slit nice and clean with your little tongue." His fingers tangle in my hair, and I know he's losing control when he thrusts into my mouth and his legs twitch. "Ah, fuck." His groan resonates in my core.

He's done letting me play and wants to take back the little control he gave me. I stare into his eyes as I slide his cock into my open mouth. The gray of his eyes darkens, and his abs become solid as I fit as much of his cock in as possible without choking.

Then he pushes farther, hitting the back of my throat, causing me to gag, and he smirks.

"Breathe, baby, breathe through your nose." He holds me in place with a hand at the back of my head, and stills while I do as he asks, then he inches farther inside. "Fuck. Fuck, it's so damn good, Hallie." His free hand grips the sheets while he raises his hips, then he withdraws, giving me a chance to catch my breath before he slams back in.

"Fuck," he growls, as I choke at the way he powers into my mouth. "So"—he lifts his hips and pushes my head down—"damn"—I gag as his fingers pinch my scalp and tears roll down my face—"good." He erupts, filling my mouth with his cum as his sharp jaw falls open, and his heavy pants fill the room. "Fuckkk."

And just like that, I realize, I own him too.

Chapter Three

Rocco

I held her in my arms all night, wishing I could prolong it. She passed out after I fucked her into the mattress and hasn't stirred since. Even when I delivered another load of cum into her swollen pussy, she slept. I fucked her slower, taking my time to relish the feeling of her surrounding me, and now as I lie with her back flush against my chest, I don't know how I will let her go, if only for a little while longer.

Having learned her Sunday routine well, I know she will be leaving me in approximately two hours, so I take advantage of the time I have with her. I press soft kisses down her spine, loving the way she arches her back. When I reach her ass, I leave a kiss on each cheek before moving lower, then nuzzle into her thick thighs. She raises her leg higher, allowing me access to her swollen pussy. I deliver a long, calculated lick, making sure to taste myself as I dip my tongue in her hole and swirl it around. Fuck, we taste good together.

She rouses from her sleep and lifts her head to stare down at me. I pause with my tongue flat, ready to lick her perfect pussy. Her chest rises and her cheeks pinken. "You're good with your tongue too." She smiles, and I nod like a fucking lapdog before going back to my pussy, then part her ass cheeks and lick her from pussy to ass.

"Oh Jesus, Rocco." She tries shooting up from the mattress, forcing me to hold her firmly in place with my hands tightening on her ass.

Pulling and pushing her, I encourage her to fuck my face and soak me with our cum. "That's it, baby, give me our cum, cover my fucking face in it."

She grinds into my mouth, then her hips buck, and I lap at her like a hungry animal, loving the fact she's now rocking her hips and riding my face. I soothe her ass with my hand, saying, "Good girl. Good fucking girl for taking what you want from your daddy." She clutches at the sheets, and when I shove two fingers inside her pussy and massage her G-spot, she clenches them perfectly, delivering me with a potent blend of our cum as she squirts over my face.

"Holy shit. What the ..." Her body tightens.

"Fuckkk." It flows from her while my fingers remain stroking deep inside her. "So good," I coo, and her heavy breaths fill the air. "So good giving Daddy a squirt." Her breath hitches and her eyes widen, and I smirk at her innocence. "Let Daddy lick you clean, Little Red." My tongue devours her pleasure, lapping at her juice with greedy hunger.

When her pussy slowly unclamps from around my fingers, I reluctantly withdraw them, and she sags against the sheets.

"I can't believe I just did that." She throws an arm over her face, and I chuckle as I crawl up her body and push her hand away, uncovering her red cheeks.

"Don't be shy, Little Red. You taste sensational."

She bites into her bottom lip, and instead of devouring it, I flip her onto her stomach fully and slap her ass.

"Hands and knees."

As she complies immediately, my cock pulsates with a need to dominate her. Lining up to her dripping hole, I drive inside her with such force I hear the air escape her lungs while her hands claw into the sheets for leverage, then I rear back and repeat the motion.

I lean over her back and wrap her hair around my fist, then let loose. All my pent-up tension and months of frustration come out in a deluge of pure control. "You belong to me." *Slam.* "You hear me?" *Thrust.* I spank her ass so hard my palm burns, and I adore the imprint left on her cheek.

"Oh god."

"Rocco or Daddy. They're the only fucking names you scream while I fuck you senseless, Little Red. You hear me?" *Smack!* "You hear me?"

"Ye-yes, Daddy."

A burst of excitement flows through me at her choice.

Daddy kink was something I never considered until I heard my brother refer to himself as that to his wife. Now all I can think about is her calling me that as I care for her, become her protector, her baby's father, her fucking everything.

"Mine!" I bellow, pumping my release deep inside her while squeezing my eyes shut and willing my seed to take root, ensuring our future together.

Hallie

Anxiety ripples through me as I slip my dress over my head. To say last night and into this morning was incredible would be an understatement, but now as I tug my dress over my hips, I slip back into my previous self, no longer a combination of wanton and submissive and back to being demure and sensible. The struggle is creeping in, weighing me down, and while I'm with Rocco, I feel nothing but alive, free.

"You're overthinking it." His voice slices through my thoughts. I know it was a one-night stand, but why does the thought of me only being that to him cause so much pain. I turn to face him, something I've avoided since sliding out of bed, hoping to leave with no exchange. After all, this was all new to me. I'd never considered having a one-night stand in my entire life.

"I'm sorry." Insecurity and embarrassment creep over me, but I pull my shoulders back, determined for him not to see the hurt I feel. "I've never done this before."

His eyebrows furrow as he searches my face, then he shocks the hell out of me by throwing the sheet off his naked body and striding toward me. My mouth falls slack at his cock standing tall and proud. The tattoos painting his body cry out for me to touch them, and I whimper at the thought of never being able to explore them, to explore him, again. His touch on my chin burns into my skin, and when his eyes hold mine hostage, my heart skips a beat. "I know. It's one of the things I like about you. But mark my words, Little Red, this isn't the end of us, this is only the beginning."

I try to make sense of his words, but the heat radiating from him clouds my mind. I open my mouth to ask him what he means, but my phone cuts through the sexual haze.

He steps back, and I wince, feeling the disappointment in my bones.

I glance at the screen and grimace. "I'm sorry. I really have to leave."

Then he takes my head in the palms of his hands and tilts me to deliver a kiss to my forehead. The touch of his soft lips seeps through my skin, warming me like never before. Which is odd, considering I've only just met the man, and when he turns his back to me, I sag, then mentally kick myself for feeling so ridiculously needy.

"I have a car waiting for you downstairs. My driver, Silas, will take you wherever you need to go." His words come out choked, as if feeling just as disappointed as I am, but that can't be, right?

I clear my throat. "Thank you." My gaze lands on his

DECEPTION

toned ass as he heads toward the bathroom, and he appears younger today than last night. When my phone vibrates again, I jump into action and grab my purse from the dresser, then head toward the door, taking with me a night I'll never forget with a man I can never have.

Rocco

The moment the apartment door closes, I slam my forehead against the bathroom door. Acting so nonchalant to her leaving me was almost my undoing. I wanted nothing more than to kidnap her, to keep her as my little red, but I've too much at stake and don't want her being caught in the crossfire.

Until my plan slips into place, I shall continue watching her from afar, and when the perfect time arises, I'll pounce, taking what's mine. All of it.

My phone rings on the bathroom counter, and I swipe at it when I see Silas's name on the screen. "Talk to me."

"Your package is collected."

My shoulders ease, knowing he's talking about Hallie. "And?"

"And just like you said, she asked to go to a pharmacy."

Hurt slices through me, and I press my hand over my

heart at the pain her actions cause. To know she's avoiding getting pregnant would probably be one man's relief, but for me, it's a nightmare.

"And you're taking her to …?"

"The store on Oak Tree, just as you requested."

I nod, overcome with emotion, then realize he won't see it. "Good. Mr. Stores is a friend of mine; he'll do what's necessary."

He will give her hormone enhancers instead of the Plan B, then encourage her to take birth control with her, while really offering her more enhancers.

"Anything else?"

"No. Just make sure she goes about her day as normal, and let me know if anything changes."

"Will do, Boss." He ends the call, and I draw my eyes up to the mirror. The scratch marks she left behind on my shoulders bring a grin to my face.

"Don't worry, Little Red. I'll take care of you, both of you." I smile, proud of the plan I've put in place.

Now I only have to wait and see it through.

Chapter Four

Rocco

Fifteen weeks and two days later ...

She reverses out of the driveway, and I smirk at the way she rushes from the house; she overslept because she stayed up late watching the last episode of *Housewives of Miami*.

When I set up the cameras in her house, I never intended them to become my salvation, but that's what happened.

My little obsession grew, and now I know what she eats, how long she sleeps, and what she wears. Daily.

Living each day in the Mafia brings violence and a fight for survival, and she's become my greatest motivation in life. I can achieve anything if I get to go home to her at night and cherish her body. I can be the man my father and La Familia need me to be with her in my thoughts. It drives me to succeed, and when I finally have her in my arms, I will truly become invincible.

My father believes women weaken you, but he hasn't found the right woman. Mine is my inspiration, my driving force, my goal, my endgame. With her by my side, I will conquer the wars that approach us, and with my child inside her, our fate will become sealed and her loyalty to me will never waiver.

I will become the man I want to be, the father I needed, and so much more. With that in mind, I lower the kickstand of my motorbike, dismount, and stride toward her house. I'm uncaring if I'm discovered by Cilla, the sweet old lady who lives across the street that I'm on a first-name basis with, or if Cliff, the mailman who delivers too early on a Saturday, sees me. They all know who I am, and I own them, so they're never an issue. Money talks for many, and they are those people.

While unlatching the gate at the side of the little house, adrenaline buzzes through me at the thought of being in her home. Our home. She just hasn't realized it yet.

Each time I enter the little white-picket-fenced house, I get the same excitable feeling thrumming through my veins, and I revel in it. My cock stiffens at the prospect of unloading, and when I draw the key from my pocket to the back door of her home, I exhale through my nose, knowing I'm about to touch the doorhandle she recently touched. My fingers curl over it, and I swear I can still feel the heat from her touch. The fingerprints she will have left behind are now on my skin, and I close my eyes, giving in to the memories of her touch and the way her soft skin felt against mine.

It's the same every time I come here, and with each day that passes, the closer I become to being a permanent fixture in her life has me riddled with hyperactivity. I won't just be touching the door handle, I'll be touching her again. I. Cannot. Fucking. Wait.

Slowly, I close the door behind me, and the smell of her home invades my senses. It calms me like no other, and I've never been able to figure out what it is specifically that has that effect on me.

Is it the sweet cinnamon from the rolls she bakes every morning? Or the smell of her coconut body lotion that floats through the air like a beacon.

Moving around the kitchen with a comfortable familiarity, I open the refrigerator and remove the huge tub of her muesli. I inwardly smile when her spoon still sits in it, and my cock jumps as I snag it out of the pot. Then I slide the spoon into my mouth and close my eyes, remembering how her tongue fought against mine until she submitted to me and allowed me the control I so desperately need.

I push the cool metal between my lips, sucking the flavor from it like I did her clit, and my cock weeps against my boxers as if it has a mind of its own and remembers the softness of her skin on my tongue.

When I'm slightly satisfied, I place the spoon back in the pot. Knowing her lips will be wrapped around the spoon and tasting me has my cock leaking in envy.

Then I turn back to the refrigerator and locate her smoothie and pull today's sedative from my jeans pocket. By the time she's done her workout this evening, the sedative will be in full effect, then she'll be fast asleep and oblivious, just how I like her.

After closing the door, I stride down the corridor with exhilaration ravishing my body. I take the stairs two at a time and ignore how the waistband on my jeans pinches the tip of my cock as I race toward her room.

Pure, unadulterated desire rushes through me when I throw open her bedroom door and the familiar scent and warmth of her wraps around me.

Unlike when I sneak into her room at night, I don't have to tiptoe around and worry about being discovered. Moving through her home so freely during the day has my body wired with a need to feel satiated, and right now, there's only one way to do just that.

Rummaging through her wash basket, I find her panties among the towel she will have used after showering this morning, and once the soft satin of the material is wrapped around my fingers, I march into the adjoining bathroom.

I take the container of coconut body lotion from the side of the bathtub and stand in front of the mirror, unscrew the lid, and lift it to my nose. My eyes roll with the scent of us combined, and the fact she has no clue heightens the thrill. The coconut lotion infused with my cum is like liquid gold and has me rushing to unbuckle my belt and pop open my jeans. The thought of her walking around all day wearing me is almost too much to

DECEPTION

bear as I tug down my boxers and let my solid cock spring out. It hits my abs, and the stickiness that leaks from my slit has my hand rushing to fist it. I lather my cock in the lotion and drive into my palm like a savage. Each thrust of my hips is like ecstasy as I unravel three days' worth of pent-up need into a pot of body lotion. I imagine her naked body standing in front of this very mirror in all her glory, her flaming-red hair shimmering beneath the lighting as she glides her hands over her pale smooth skin. Unwittingly rubbing in my cum and allowing it to seep into her bloodstream adds fuel to my raging fire.

The way her tits sway as she coats herself in me has my balls aching.

"Fuck, baby, you like me covering you, don't you?" I pick up pace and thrust harder, dipping the tip of my cock into the pot. "Fuck, yes," I growl as I grind my teeth.

My hair falls over my eyes as sweat beads on my forehead, and the muscles in my back strain as tingles shoot up my spine, then my fist works quicker. Choking, I come hard, my body burning with fervor as I unload my warm cum into the pot. I squeeze the tip of my cock, drawing out the pleasure and ensuring every drop blends with the lotion.

As I come down from my orgasm, my chest heaves. I tuck my spent cock into my boxers, then use my finger to mix my cum into the lotion, providing her with the perfect combination to cover her sacred skin.

When I withdraw my hand, I lift my T-shirt and rub the remaining lotion over my scorched heart, bringing with it comfort. I won't have to wait too much longer; in three days' time, my plan comes together and brings an unbridled beginning with it.

Lounging on her bed with my head resting against her pillow, I scroll through the footage of her leaving the house this morning and smile. She's fucking adorable when she's flustered, and I cannot wait to see if her ass turns the same sexy shade of red as her cheeks do when I spank her time and time again. Her work attire fits her perfectly, but I grind my teeth at knowing someone else is benefiting from seeing her dressed like that. Not for long, though. When I reveal myself, I'll get to witness her dressed like this every damn day, up close and personal, and I cannot fucking wait for it.

When I need somewhere to feel calm, this is where I come. She's the eye of my storm, my safe place when I'm surrounded by such chaos and destruction. She's my home, and I cannot wait to be in it, literally.

Full of contentment, I breathe in the scent of her shampoo on the fabric of the pillow and savor it, remembering her resting her head on my chest, completely spent and at my mercy.

The sound of a car coming up the drive has me pulling up the external camera, and my heart misfires when it's her. "Oh shit." My pulse races with my mind as I wonder why she's home so soon.

She throws open the car door as I slide off the bed and dart my eyes around the room to look for a place to hide. My eyes latch onto the window, yet I can't bring myself to use it—not when there's a chance we can be in the same room together again. The thought stirs my cock back to life.

The car door slams, and her heels click against the pathway. What the hell am I thinking?

The veins on my temple pulsate, and I freeze like a startled animal caught in the headlights.

Then the turn of her key has me snapping out of it and my feet moving as I finally decide to hide under her bed. My body hits the floor as her front door closes and the soft sound of her voice filters through. "I don't know how the hell it happened. I was in a rush, and I misjudged the placement of the cup, knocking the lid off in the process."

"Are you okay?" Sharna replies. After spending so much time analyzing Hallie's days, I've become accustomed to her best friend too. They're on speakerphone as her footsteps move closer to the bedroom, causing my heart to hammer and my cock to thicken. Yet when I process what Sharna is saying, panic barrels into me. Is Hallie hurt?

My spine straightens and I'm two seconds away from revealing myself when the bedroom door flies open, taking my breath with it.

"I'm fine. It was just iced tea." My shoulders sag as she continues on. "It's going to be a bastard to get out of my dress, though." She giggles, and my lip quirks at her cuteness.

"Okay, as long as you're okay. Don't worry about Tony. Show him a bit of cleavage, and he'll be fine."

My molars grind. *Show him fucking cleavage? What the actual fuck, Sharna?*

"Eww," Hallie responds, settling my immediate anger.

Sharna laughs. "Speak later."

"Bye." Hallie throws her phone onto the bed and swings open the bathroom door. Her reflection in the bathroom mirror steals the air from my lungs.

Fifteen fucking weeks since I've been as close as I am right now—awake, at least. Yet I still can't touch her, and my god, she's just as beautiful. She has an ambiance about her that settles me, a kindness like I've never known and a sexiness almost alien to me. She tilts her hips from side to side, scrutinizing the splash marks on her dress, and I almost whimper at the thought of my cum marking her the same way. Splashes of my glory would look impeccable on her while she pleads for more and I deliver it tenfold, making her Daddy's little cum slut. The head of my cock leaks pre-cum, and I shift uncomfortably.

She huffs, breaking me from my thoughts, then grabs the hem of the dress and whips it over her head, sending her curls flowing down her back. When she drops her dress to the floor and reveals her red lacy bra and matching panties, my mouth drops open as air whooshes from my lungs. Holy. Fucking. Shit.

Pain throbs in my balls, pulling me out of my haze, and when her eyes latch onto the pot of coconut lotion, I bite into my lower lip to prevent me from whimpering my approval.

Please. Please fucking do it.

My breath catches in my throat as she lifts the pot.

Oh, fuck yes.

She unscrews the lid, and I've no choice but to undo my jeans at the same time. Knowing my girl is about to cover herself in my cum sends a guttural need rushing through me, leaving me uncaring if she hears the sound of me jerking my cock.

I wrap my tattooed hand around my thickness, and my mouth waters as I pump it, watching with avid satisfaction as she rubs the lotion into her stomach. She hums a soft tune as her hand moves farther north toward her heavy tits, and my hips buck as I fuck my hand desperately. "Please, baby," I whisper as I make out the darkness of her peaked nipple. My mouth waters as I imagine locking my lips around it, milking it while I pump my cock and feed from her.

Fucking please rub it on them too. Coat yourself with my cum and play with your nipples for Daddy while he strokes himself.

Her breath hitches, and I think she's going to dip her hand into her bra, but she doesn't, and I choke back my disappointment, but then she coats her fingers and massages it into the swell of her tits. They bounce with each touch, and I practically combust. My cock launches ropes of pre-cum, providing the perfect lubricant, but all I want is to punish her for the action because her touch would mean so much more.

She lifts her leg onto the counter, and I can't help the sound of satisfaction that leaves my throat at seeing her so exposed. The thin fabric of her lace panties covering her little pussy lips has my orgasm rushing toward me. Her fingers shift closer to her pussy, and my abs contract to rein in my orgasm, but she breezes over her bikini line, and I long to lick the lotion from between her legs. She looks exquisite with her high heels on, in nothing but her lingerie. Every inch of her is utter beauty, and when she bends forward, giving me a front-row seat to her tits, I come undone. Pleasure zips up my spine, and I bite into my lip to prevent the roar desperate to release from deep inside my chest, piercing the skin and squeezing my eyes closed as the hot cum covers my hand and T-shirt.

When I finally open my eyes and tilt my head toward her, she's rushing around the bathroom, then disappears into her closet. She comes back out moments later fully dressed, then breezes through the room and closes the door behind her, taking my comfort with her. I finally exhale the breath I've been holding and chuckle. "So fucking close, Rocco." I grin. Her car starts, and I slide out from beneath the bed.

"So fucking close I can almost taste it."

Chapter Five

Rocco

A loud huff leaves my father. "I don't know why you're bothering with school." He shoves another spoon of granola into his mouth. "You don't need it." As he points his spoon toward me, I take a sip of my orange juice, then lift my shoulder, unwilling to respond.

Not today, at least. Today will be a good day.

It's been weeks since we settled issues at one of the clubs, and I'm unwilling to wait any longer. I need her. My body craves her, and the pressure my father is putting on me is becoming unavoidable. So today is the day.

And I cannot fucking wait.

"School is for wasters." He chides, and I almost choke on his words. Pretty damn sure most parents wouldn't agree.

"You like your accounts in order, and I like to keep

tabs on what's happening." Lies, all lies. "School helps with that." My brother Tommy does our family accounts, even when he was meant to be absent from the family. Rafael, our oldest brother, threw work his way. Papa mumbles, and I take that as his approval.

I like to cut up our enemies and destroy anyone that gets in my way. I've become the perfect Mafia son over the years. My father's brutal parentage has crafted me well, leaving me unhinged at best.

Although my father has never been abusive toward me and my brothers, the demands he puts on us are violent and catalytic to a child's mind. We never had a normal family upbringing. None of us ever had a mother figure growing up, and whenever any of us would become close to one of the numerous nannies, he would abruptly cut them from our lives. It's part of the reason I wonder if that's why I'm so drawn to Hallie's soft nature; I've been void of it my entire upbringing.

"You have an event coming up with the Harrington girl." He waves his arm around as if trying to think of the Harrington girl's name.

"Kimberly?" I offer. "The girl you're forcing me to marry. Or was it Livvy? I can't remember."

He balks at my words, and I sit back in my chair, crossing my arms over my chest as I stare at him.

His eyes hold mine. "Doesn't matter whatever her fucking name is."

I sneer. Of course it doesn't matter; she's as much a pawn in this as I am. I also know her name is Olivia.

DECEPTION

"Don't start acting like a child, Rocco. It's a means to an end, that's all."

Anger rushes up my spine, and I sit forward. "The end being what, exactly? We have money, we have alliances, what more could we possibly fucking need?"

"Her father's a—"

"Jackass. Her father's a jackass judge."

Scoffing again, he shakes his head. "Just continue the fucking bloodline, will you? And do as you've been asked. Marry her and get her pregnant."

"And you think he's going to be happy? I stick my dick in other women while his little princess waits at home for me to get her knocked up?"

"He'll get used to it." He shrugs like the heartless piece of shit I know him to be.

"What, like you did?" I spit back, referring to the women who have scorned my father. His steely eyes snap up to mine, and he glares at me with a threat of violence. I'm past caring, and I'm pissed he's ruining my day.

The tension is interrupted by the horn of a car outside, and my shoulders drop while my father's attention is pulled over my shoulder toward the front window. "Why is there a little punk collecting you for school?"

I choke on a laugh at his reference to Matt, my best friend. "Because it's what normal schoolkids do."

He narrows his eyes on me. "You're not a normal schoolkid."

"Don't I fucking know it," I grumble as I push back on my chair and snag a slice of toast from my plate.

"Rocco, I don't know what the fuck you're playing at,

but I know we don't have time for this shit." He glares as I round his chair and head toward the door, unprepared to listen to another damn word that comes out of his mouth.

"Stay out of my fucking business," I spit back as I stride through it.

"Jesus," my father mutters as I slam the door behind me and plaster on a smile I feel deep in my bones. Spending time with Matt makes me feel fucking normal, and knowing I'm about to reveal myself makes me feel sensational.

Matt's eyes bug out as I make my way toward the car, and I can't help the chuckle that rumbles in my chest.

As soon as I open the car door and slide into the car seat, his questions start. "What the fuck, man? You're loaded." He throws his hand out toward the line of sports cars.

"I am."

He glances around the expansive grounds. "Like really fucking loaded." His eyebrows rise, and his jaw practically falls to the floor.

"Yep." I pop the p, with a wide grin.

As if seeing me for the first time, he slowly trails his eyes over me from head to toe. My combat boots are unlaced, and my signature ripped jeans, white T-shirt, and leather jacket are all in place. Nope, I definitely don't give off the rich-kid vibe with my appearance. There sure as shit isn't anything preppy about me.

He shakes his head. "You never said you had money." His tone is laced in hurt, and I can understand that. Until today, I've kept Matt as far away from my home life as possible. Hell, even my father never knew I had a friend from outside of our world, and for good reason too. There's no way in hell I wanted Matt to get wrapped up in my chaos. My world is dangerous and not one I want to expose him to unless necessary.

"That a problem?" I counter.

His mouth snaps shut, and he shakes his head. "Nuh-no. Of course not, it's just ... you don't look like the kids at my school. Hell, you don't even look like a kid." He waves his hand in my direction.

A loud chuckle erupts from me. He's not lying. I look nothing like a damn kid, and I'm proud of the fact. My father insisted on making men out of his sons early in our lives, and that included a range of activities that would be frowned upon in everyday life. My body is covered in tattoos, my kill count is ostentatious, my behavior is unpredictable, at best, and the brutal sexual tendencies I attempt to keep hidden are slowly unraveling—because of her.

When I first met Matt, he was being bullied in a coffee shop. Some jerks at his school had surrounded a table he'd set up as a study area. I watched from the doorway as one swiped his book onto the floor while another lifted Matt's hot chocolate above his head, and I saw red. Before I knew what I was doing, I was striding through the shop at lightning speed to save a kid who was a lot younger and smaller than them from being ridiculed and damaged any further.

The hot chocolate was knocked out of the punk's hand when I delivered a swift punch to his jaw that sent him falling to the floor with a heavy thud. Then, with my combat boot on his face, I stared off with the other two jerks who stupidly decided to move toward me. In a flash, I withdrew my knife and threw it into one of the guy's thighs. He went down squealing like a pig while the other guy saw the same fate as his friend beneath my boot. Only he knocked over a tray of drinks on the opposite table as he went down, leaving him soaked, much like they'd intended on doing to my new friend who watched me with wide, innocent eyes.

I spun the chair around, dropped myself in it, and asked my new buddy if he could assist me with my math homework. He nodded frantically, making me chuckle. He had nothing to be nervous about; this little guy needed a friend, and I needed him. We've been close ever since.

"I can't believe you're moving to my school, man. This is insane!" He grins, showing off his perfectly white teeth no longer housed in braces.

"I know." I smirk while sinking further into his car seat.

Pulling away from my house, he continues to shake his head. "You have an armed guard at a security post?" He nods toward one of our men as we drive past, and his pale, stunned expression has me chuckling.

"It's not fucking funny, Roc." He shoves me playfully. "What the fuck, man?"

With a smirk, I lift my shoulder. "I wanted to remain incognito."

DECEPTION

"Incog-fucking-nito?" His mouth falls open. "Just who the hell are you and your family?"

"The Mafia," I state as my spine straightens, awaiting his reaction.

He swallows thickly, and I wait on tenterhooks for his response. "Okay. Well, my parents are going to lose their shit. Just so you know."

My grin spreads across my face. "I'm counting on it." His eyes narrow. "At least they know I have your back." I shrug.

He nods. "Right. I mean, we don't have to mention the Mafia thing to them straight away, right?"

I shrug. "Guess not." It's no big deal to me whether he tells them.

"My mom is pretty desperate to meet you, and she makes a mean lasagna. You have to try that before this"—he waves his hand between us—"all goes to shit."

I balk at his words and slouch back into the seat, then my heart races as I calculate that we're twelve minutes away from my destiny—her.

Chapter Six

Hallie

I wake up to the familiar scent that has haunted my dreams since that one night with him. It's weird how, after all this time, I still sense his presence.

The way I dream about how he touched me and worshipped my body should be criminal. Hell, it could be considered obsessive. Maybe it's because he's the first person I've been with since Gerrard?

The thoughts of doing those things with anyone but him makes my stomach twist in knots, yet he made no move to take my phone number. Sharna might be right. Maybe we should return to the club and seek him out, but the thought of doing that and risking seeing him with someone else makes me want to throw up.

Nope, definitely won't be doing that.

I need to get over it—or under it, like Sharna suggests. Maybe it's time to date again.

Tony in the sports department has asked me out numerous times, and he's not bad to look at, but he has a desperate look in his eyes that screams I killed his puppy every time I say I'm not ready to date.

Staring into the mirror, I glance over myself one last time. My red hair glistens in the sun, and my skin glows like never before. The way he called me Little Red set my body ablaze with a potent fire I wish would burn for an eternity.

Since that night, it's like Rocco unleashed something inside of me that made me feel alive. He delivered me with so many compliments that confidence oozed from me. I felt his need for me in my bones and my pussy too. His hungry eyes were full of sincerity, and after years of being suppressed, I finally released my inhibitions and became the woman I want to be.

I became me.

Heat travels over my face at the way my thoughts have once again returned to him, and I shake my head, then grab my laptop bag and slip my feet into my pumps. Even with my heels on, I'm still small, but at my normal height of five foot two, they fill me with assurance as I deliver lessons to my students. With that thought in mind, I stride toward my door toward my working day.

It's time I move on with my life, and maybe it's time I move on from him too.

Chapter Seven

Rocco

Adrenaline surges through my veins as I make my way toward my first lesson.

I've waited for this day for years, and today, I can finally reveal myself. Today, my little red will learn who haunts her dreams, who owns every inch of her body. Whose cock she took so willingly without the knowledge of who I am, what I am and, more importantly, my age.

I swagger past the students in the corridor with a cocky confidence, ignoring the cheerleaders admiring me and the disapproving looks of the jocks who quickly turn their backs when I return their glares. As I head into class, eagerness vibrates through my body like an addict about to get his next fix. Finding an empty desk, I throw my backpack to the floor, drop down into the chair, and widen my legs.

The moment she steps foot in class, I feel her, and the hairs on the back of my neck stand to attention. The air is stolen from my lungs as I raise my head to face her. With my heart pounding and my mouth as dry as a desert, her beauty steals the ability for me to function. Although, my cock doesn't have an issue. The fucker pokes me in the stomach, reminding me I'm alive.

My gaze roams over her, taking in every inch of her delectable body. The memory of her curves has my cock leaking and my fingers twitching to touch her, and when she parts her lips to speak, the reminder of her mouth stretched to capacity taking my cock flashes before me. "Welcome everyone, my name is Ms. Davis." And like that, anger surges from deep inside me because the woman before me has his surname, not mine. "And I will be your English teacher this year."

The need to make her mine at whatever costs is at its highest. I need to move this thing between us forward, and now that everything has quietened at the club, I have the perfect opportunity to do so.

There's nothing stopping me anymore.

Not even her.

Chapter Eight

Hallie

The moment I stepped into the office this morning, Tony thrust a coffee into my hand while his gaze roamed over my body appreciatively. Yet not one ounce of my body responded. Not like it did to *his* heated stare.

I mentally chastise myself for the hundredth time today. *Stop thinking about him, Hallie.*

"So, how about it?" He nudges me with his elbow.

My eyes flick over his face. "Huh?" I mean, sure, he's cute, but he's also very clean cut. Like my ex and so unlike the man who haunts my every thought.

I shake my head and try again, taking in the small dimples when he smiles and the way his blue eyes light up with kindness as he stares into my eyes. "I asked you out to dinner. How about it? Can you do tomorrow? We could grab pizza and catch up at Lance's restaurant on Brick Street."

My words won't come out as my gaze roams over him. His hair is cropped short at the sides and longer on top, styled perfectly. His crisp light-blue shirt is open at the top, exposing his pristine bronzed skin, not a tattoo in sight, and my fingers don't itch to explore it. He wears slacks like Gerrard, and his brown shoes are polished to perfection.

"I'm not sure," I mumble.

He chuckles, and it does nothing for me while I remain rigid on the spot. "I know you're apprehensive about the dating scene, Hallie. But come on, it's dinner, no commitment, I swear. Just two friends getting to know each other outside of this." He looks over his shoulder toward the mayhem of the teacher's lounge, and I laugh and finally agree.

"Okay."

He rears back slightly and searches my face with wide eyes. "Yeah?"

I bite into my lip and nod, and the way his eyes dance as an excitable expression covers his face has me smiling back at him. He is kind of cute.

"Okay. I'll text you the time." His smile grows wider, and I already regret agreeing.

"Okay," I mumble.

As he steps closer like he's going to pull me toward him, I retract, causing a laugh to rumble from him as he throws his hands up. "Okay, I'll break down those walls, Hallie. Trust me." He winks as he backs away, and the smile I plastered on my face falls as he turns. In all honesty, I don't want the carefully constructed walls breaking down.

I want them smashed the way Rocco did.

Then he turns his head over his shoulder. "Oh, you have a new student today too. Check your email, and good luck." He grimaces, making me react with a genuine chuckle for the first time.

I lift my laptop bag to my shoulder and throw open the office door and make my way toward class.

The hallways are chaos as usual, but as the bell rings, it dissipates and silence fills the corridors, bringing me solace as I make my way toward the first lesson of the day.

This is what I love, outside of my home and family. This is my passion. Something Gerrard never understood. I insisted on making a career for myself and not depending on him. Something he's always resented me for.

Over the years, he humored me, allowing me to pursue the relevant college courses, but whenever I mentioned actually working, he balked, telling me I was where I was always meant to be. At his side, being the perfect housewife. He never had any intentions of letting me thrive outside of his ridiculous ideology.

I throw open the classroom door, and the hushed voices of my students send a wave of confidence through me. They respect me, simply because I respect them, and with that mutual respect, it has created a relationship I can be proud of.

Some students in this class are new to me this year,

but I intend to build the same relationship and reputation with them as I have since I arrived here.

I place my coffee on the desk and unpack my laptop, then start it up as I lift my head to address the room.

"Welcome everyone, my name is Ms. Davis. I will be your English teacher this year." They hang on my every word, and I bask in it. "Some of you have transferred to my class, and I'm honored to have you here, but I also need you to know this class is not going to be an easy ride. You will be expected to put in the work to achieve your expected grades. If you're not willing to do so, there's the door." I point toward the door. "Don't be afraid to use it, because I won't be." I clap my hands. "Now that that's out the way, let's get down to business. We have a new student to welcome." I glance down at the name sitting in my email and jolt as my eyes register his first name. Can the universe really hate me so much he named a kid after the guy who haunts my dreams? I shake my head to banish the ridiculous notion and scan over the classroom in search of the boy in question. "Rocco Marino."

All eyes turn toward a desk at the back of the room, and when I zero in on the student, the air is stolen from my lungs. My organs twist to the point of pain because staring back at me is the man who worshipped my body and delivered me so many orgasms I collapsed. The same man who unlocked something inside of me I never knew existed, and I want to devour but also swipe the cocky smirk he's wearing from his smug, edible face.

He's a student.

Holy shit, he's my student.

Chapter Nine

Rocco

When her gaze finally lands on mine, my body heats with need. Fuck, she's beautiful. The way her startled hazel eyes widen, her face flames, and her lips part has a rumble of laughter erupting from me.

Fuck me, she's adorable when she's in shock, and I want nothing more than to shove my tongue between those plush lips of hers while holding her face in the palms of my hands, giving her no choice but to accept me.

Whispers ripple through the classroom, and I want to banish them in order to protect her, so I become what she needs me to be—the perfect student.

"Here," I grunt out, and delight in the shiver that takes over her, then I dart my eyes away, as much as it pains me to.

I can still feel her eyes on me as she clears her throat,

then begins outlining the course for this year. Quite simply, I don't care. The only reason I chose this class was to be near her, to be in her proximity. To invade every part of her life until she's no choice but to crave me like I do her.

Trying to infiltrate a school was much harder than I first anticipated, and the only feasible way to do it was to become a student, so here I am.

My father's right. I need none of this, but what I do need is her.

And if she works here without me in her presence, she will always have the opportunity to live a life outside of me, and I refuse to let that continue any longer. Sure, I don't want to become the same as her ex, but the man had a point; he just went about it the wrong way.

Not me, though. As soon as my girl agrees to my terms, then I will be much more lenient to agree to hers, and it's not lost on me how much she enjoys this career. She exudes confidence and, in my research, I discovered just how much she helps her students succeed.

She's phenomenal, and I'd never take this away from her, but that doesn't mean I can't use it to get what I want too.

Hallie

Somehow, I get through the lesson, but my mind keeps replaying the moment I laid eyes on him, sitting there with a knowing smirk on his handsome face, almost taunting me.

I avoided looking at him as much as possible. He didn't engage with the lesson, something I was grateful for, yet I would normally call a student out on it and question them for their lack of engagement. Not today. Today, I don't have it in me. I just can't wait to get the hell out of here and try to figure out how badly I screwed up by giving myself over to him.

Standing, I plaster on a smile for the students as they filter out of the classroom. Every hair on my body stands on end with him still in the classroom. I can feel him like I do every morning, as if he's burrowed beneath my skin.

My blood boils with a rage at the injustice, then I snap my head up as he saunters toward me like the predator he is. I swallow harshly under his scrutiny as his gray eyes fill with the same hunger I encountered only weeks ago.

"Little Red." He smiles, and I hate how my body reacts to him as he licks his lips.

"What are you doing here, Rocco?" My heart thunders in my chest and my legs tremble at the use of his name.

His lips quirk, and I grind my teeth. Is this a joke to him?

"I'm a student." He smiles broadly.

Hearing him say the words, despite me already knowing, has my body jolting, and I grip my desk to stabilize myself.

Oh god.

My chest heaves as panic sets in.

Oh, shit.

Reality hits me hard as my world crumbles around me. Everything I worked hard for diminished on a single word—student.

I mean, is he even legal?

"Shhh, calm down, Little Red." His hand settles over my cheek, and I feel his touch deep in my core. "I think you're having a panic attack. Breathe, baby, breathe through your nose." His lip twitches.

The familiarity of his words is like electricity firing through my veins, sending a blaze of fury to snap me from my meltdown. I knock his hands away and step back, unsure of how he even ended up so close to me to begin with.

"Get off me. What the hell are you doing?" I snap,

and he rubs his hand over his jaw, but I don't miss the tic in his temple or the glare he slices toward me, something I've never encountered with him before. A pit of dread settles in my stomach at the realization of not knowing him at all.

He takes a deep breath and fixes his eyes to hold mine. "What I'm doing is taking what I want." My eyes dart over his face. "And what I want, Little Red, is you." The darkness in his tone sends a bolt of fear through me.

My heart skips a beat, and I tell myself it's due to the horror of his admission, nothing else. He steps forward, forcing me to step back until my ass is flush against the desk, and he cages me in, his hand on either side of me as he stares into my soul, seeing the want and need I've been craving.

"Are you eighteen?" I mumble, my words sounding like a plea more than anything else.

"I am."

I blow out a breath of relief while my heart hammers precariously.

He reaches out and toys with a strand of my hair. "You gave me the best birthday gift I could have asked for."

His words stun me, and I struggle to speak. "Oh god." I slap a hand over my mouth as I realize we fucked on his birthday. Self-loathing hits me like a Mack truck as sickness swirls in my stomach.

I screwed a student.

I fucked an eighteen-year-old and, even worse, I've been lusting after him ever since.

Chapter Ten

Rocco

Her reaction is priceless. She's conflicted; I can see it and practically smell the confliction she's emitting, and I swell with pride over it. Fear flickers in her eyes, and I delight in the reaction. It makes my cock hard. I will prove to her that where I'm concerned, she should have none.

My poor little red is stunned, panicking, and no doubt punishing herself because she wants me.

I've read her text messages; each one she sends Sharna, craving me as much as I crave her, and now that she finally gets me, she knows she shouldn't want me. A double-edged sword so sharp it's slicing her morals down the middle.

Slowly, like dealing with a coiled snake, I remove her fingers from her mouth, and holding them in my hand sends a flood of arousal leaking into my boxers.

My cock has been perpetually hard all morning, and I want nothing more than to slide into her wet little pussy, delivering the final part of my plan.

Then I move our hands toward her pencil skirt, the one I spent the lesson avoiding. Knowing everyone gets to witness my girl's assets had me teetering on the edge, but I remained in control.

"Ro—"

"Shh, you don't want me to tell anyone about us, do you?"

Her face pales, and a sob catches in her throat as she shakes her head.

"Then let me play," I say with a warning glare. "Let me show you how good these little fingers can work in my hand. Let me guide you to your little cunt, Hal." Her breath hitches, spurring me on, and I lick my lips as I move our hands beneath the fabric and trail them up toward her panties.

"Roc—" I slice my gaze toward hers, and she snaps her mouth shut.

"Good girl. Let me show you." I graze the lace of her panties, and her free hand falls against my T-shirt as I guide her fingers toward her wet pussy. She twists her hand into the material, clinging to me as I use her fingers to stroke over her wet pussy lips. "Be a good girl, Little Red, and let me play with you." I work over her clit, stroking back and forth. "Let me play with my girl's dripping pussy. Let me make you feel good."

Her eyes become hooded, and I swear I feel her need for me in my balls, the ache in them bordering on painful.

DECEPTION

"Ple ..." I encourage her to press on her clit while my thumb moves toward her hole, and my body preens in the wetness gathering there. I pump it inside her, and her nails dig into my chest as I curve my digit to hit the spot that drives her wild.

"You beg so beautifully, Little Red," I whisper against her hair. "Come on Daddy's hand, coat him with your cum, Little Red."

She chokes on her scream as she buries her face into my T-shirt. Her small pussy clings to my thumb, and I barely hang on long enough to see her through her orgasm.

The sound of students outside of the door has her becoming rigid at my touch, and I have no choice but to pull back, pissed when she blows out a heavy sigh.

Bringing my thumb to my mouth, I make a show of sucking her sweet pussy juice from me, and our eyes remain connected as the sexual longing fills the air.

"I'm coming for you, Little Red. You're mine." I wink as I pick my backpack up off the floor. Her eyes burn a hole in my back as I head for the door, with my cock as hard as granite, but I choose to ignore it. Pretty fucking soon, I will live inside her pussy.

I slip my fingers into my mouth, and the taste of her essence spikes my obsession as I make a detour toward the parking lot. If I can't come inside my woman, I can make sure I come in her proximity.

Chapter Eleven

Hallie

I barely slept a wink all night, tossing and turning, self-loathing clawing at my skin. He's my student, and I'm his teacher. He's eighteen and fucked me with his fingers, and worse, I let him.

Last night, I contemplated texting Sharna but deleted each message I typed, too scared to admit how I feel for someone so young—my student, for Christ's sake.

What the hell have I done? I scrub a hand down my face and drag myself out of bed with a heavy sigh, then head toward the shower.

The familiar scent I've become accustomed to lingers in the air, and I swear it's him I smell, yet I know it's impossible.

Stepping into the shower, I switch on the jets and close my eyes. After adding some shower gel to my sponge, I wash my body clean, hoping to rid myself of the sins I've participated in.

That can't happen again. Ever.

I've worked too damn hard to risk my career and the reputation of my family for a fling. I'm not that person. I turn off the taps and step out, then wrap a towel around myself and head back into the bedroom to get ready for the day ahead.

My phone buzzes on the mattress, and I pick it up, then grimace at the name on the screen.

> Tony: Don't forget we're meeting up for dinner after work. 6pm at Lances.

Shit. Could this day get any worse?

> Me: Okay.

Tony shoves another slice of pizza into his mouth, and I cringe at the chunk of cheese hanging from the tips of his fingers as he continues to talk with his mouth full.

"So, I said, look, just because you're the principal"—cheese splutters out of his mouth, and I rear back—"doesn't mean you get to choose the syllabus in my lesson without my consent." I nod while turning my attention away from him, unable to watch him eat and talk any longer.

"Consent is everything, don't you think, Hallie?"

My mouth parts as Rocco's smooth voice has me

darting my gaze up toward his blazing eyes, then back toward Tony. Oh shit, he's here. This can't be happening. Panic flashes through me, causing my lungs to constrict.

Rocco stands above him and rests a hand on Tony's shoulder, then he turns his head to stare at Rocco with wide eyes. "Wh-who are you?"

"I'm someone who wants to speak with Hallie in private," he grits out as his gray eyes darken, making me swallow at the deadly threat behind them.

"Oh, but we're eating." Tony gestures toward his plate, ignorant to Rocco's threatening demeanor.

Rocco leans over and tightens his grip on his shoulder, his tattoos moving under the tension. "I suggest you leave, right. Fucking. Now." Each word is deadly, laced with a violent threat.

I clear my throat. "Tony, could you please just give me a minute? Perhaps you could get me another drink?" I nod toward my empty glass.

His shell-shocked face turns to mine, and when he finally nods, relief floods me. He pushes back in his chair and stumbles. Rocco barely gives him room to leave, and Tony grumbles under his breath as he heads toward the bar. "M-my pizza best not be cold."

Rocco slides into his chair, and I feel the weight of his stare in my soul. "A date?" He arches an eyebrow. "I had my fingers in your pussy, and you go on a date with another man?" His jaw sharpens, and the hatred radiates from him.

"It isn't a date. It's dinner," I snap.

He leans closer. "It's a fucking date, Hallie. A date

with what's mine." My breath hitches and my pulse races. Why the hell do I like the thought of him claiming me so much? What the hell is wrong with me? The insanity behind the thought unsettles me, but still, I know it to be true. I can feel it in my bones.

The tendons on his neck protrude as if he's fighting to remain calm. "You're to leave. Right fucking now." He stabs his finger on the table.

"What if I don't want to?" I raise my chin.

"Then I'll slit his throat and fuck you in his blood while the entire restaurant watches, Little Red." He drags a calculated finger over his lip, and I can't help but lick my own. "I'll open your cunt nice and wide while my cum drips from you, letting everyone know who owns you. Hm, that would be perfect, if you ask me." His tongue darts out over his lip as if contemplating doing just that.

My lips part, but as footsteps approach the table, I push back on my chair.

"I'm sorry, Tony. I have a family emergency. I have to leave."

"Oh, he's family?" He waves a hand toward Rocco.

I part my lips to respond, but Rocco snags hold of my arm and walks us away from the table. "That's right, motherfucker. I'm family. I'm her fucking daddy."

My mouth falls open, and I will the floor to open and swallow me whole, but something tells me Rocco would pull me out kicking and screaming while declaring I'm his.

DECEPTION

The rough grip he has on me tightens as he marches us out the door. "Now Daddy needs to punish you."

His threat is ominous and laced with a promise I want him to explore. I hate myself for it because I sure as hell shouldn't crave my student's depravity like this. I should be trying to pull him into the light, not be drawn into his darkness.

Rocco

I followed her home. She doesn't realize it yet, but she's about to.

When I marched her out of the restaurant, I allowed her to tug her arm from me as she rushed toward her car. She scrambled to strap herself into the car before she glanced at me one final time and started up the engine.

Little did she know I was only moments behind her. All part of my plan while I use the time to calm down.

I've never felt as unhinged as I did at seeing her sitting opposite the chump, who is about to realize he doesn't get to touch what doesn't belong to him.

Ever.

I park my bike opposite her house and follow the path around the back, then slip inside her house. It does little to calm the raging storm inside me, and each step up her stairs only aggravates me further.

Does she like him?

Does her pussy get wet for him?

Why the fuck did I wait so long to infiltrate the school? She could have been fucking him there, and I wouldn't be aware of it. Although I've read all the messages between her and Sharna that assured me she had zero interest in the punk, I'm consumed with ravenous jealousy.

I throw open her bedroom door, and her head darts up off the bed as a shell-shocked scream leaves her.

"What the hell, Rocco?"

"Do you like him?"

Her wide eyes make my cock ache to fill her mouth until she gags, forcing her green specks to sparkle as tears fill her vision.

"Answer me!" I bellow.

She shakes her head. "No. No, I swear it."

I pace the room as my fury rivals the highest level on the Richter scale. My hands ache from being balled into fists, and my heart thunders with the way my blood pumps with savagery as I tug on my hair.

I shouldn't have given anyone the opportunity to take what's mine. I should have become a student sooner. "What the fuck do I have to do, huh?" I spin and face her. "What do I have to do to make people realize you're mine?" I'm not surprised I don't get an answer when her face is frozen with a stunned expression.

"Do I have to piss on what's mine like a goddamn dog?" Her mouth falls open, and the need to stuff it has me popping open the buttons of my jeans as an eagerness to follow through with my suggestion rushes up my spine. "Yeah, that's what I need to do." I nod as the deranged notion morphs into a powerful force. "I need to piss on what's mine. Then they'll all know you belong to me." I sound unhinged, and that's just how I feel.

"Rocco?" Her eyes bulge, but it's not with fear. Intrigue, maybe?

My cock is semihard as I pull it from my jeans.

"Holy shit. You-you can't be serious." She holds my gaze.

"Deadly." Then I piss on the bed, and it splashes her bare legs, causing an intense feeling of power to slam into me, especially when she doesn't move. She remains still, and that gives me the confidence to aim myself higher, covering her white blouse with my piss, and my chest rises with exhilaration. Covering her with me, my warmth, my possession.

Her blouse becomes see-through, and my cock stiffens when her nipples become visible beneath her wet clothes. Holy fuck, she's fucking beautiful.

My eyes close as I try to banish the way my pleasure is escalating. Never did I think I would be into this, but fuck me, I am.

A low whimper has my eyes snapping open, and arousal zips up my spine on her parted lips. A flush creeps over her face when my piss lands on her cleavage and runs toward her tits. "Fuck," I heave as I tilt my head back and squeeze my eyes closed again. My cock stiffens in my palm, throbbing in the degradation of my action. Her compliance makes it almost impossible to keep the steady stream going. "Fuck, Little Red."

"Holy shit," she whispers, as if mesmerized, and I

snap my eyes open to stare at her. My piss comes to a stop at the sound of our labored breaths filling the room, and our stares remain locked.

The atmosphere becomes electric, and I remain frozen, unable to comprehend where my deluge of psychosis came from and why she's still sitting there looking like I hung the moon and stars for her. Before I have a chance to speak, she lunges forward and takes my cock in her small hand. My balls tighten and my heart skips a beat when her tongue flickers over the remnants of my piss mixed with a bead of pre-cum. "Holy fuck, Little Red. Holy fuck." My eyes roll at the degradation my little red gets off on.

Absolutely perfect.

I clear my throat when she slides me inside her slick mouth. "That's right. Lick me clean, Little Red. Lick Daddy clean from the chaos." I practically hum in contentment as she submits to my commands, proving how truly perfect we are for one another.

She's the gas that lights my fire, and together, we become an inferno of insanity.

Chapter Twelve

Hallie

Last night, not long after Rocco came down my throat, his phone rang. Then he groaned and began pacing before finally spinning to face me and telling me he had to leave. I saw the reluctance in his eyes, and disappointment filled my own.

I can't even begin to explain the craziness of what ensued in my bedroom, but watching him so riled, so possessed with jealousy that he pissed on me to make a filthy point of the ownership he craves had wetness drenching my panties.

I've never witnessed such a feral action, and I crave more of it.

When he left, he took a part of me with him, and as much as I shouldn't want him, I can't help it.

My cheeks heat as I try not to think about last night again, then I glance back up to where his stare sears into mine. I should not be thinking of him, of us, while I'm teaching, but that's exactly where my mind is.

The class is unaware of this magnetic pull between us as they work on their assignments, and there's no way I can stop this with the insane attraction I have for him.

He curls his lip into a knowing smile, and when the bell sounds, he remains unperturbed while everyone packs away their bags and clears the room for their next class.

My heart beats faster with each calculated step he takes toward me, and his grin grows wider.

When he's finally at my desk, I feel like my legs are about to give way. "Can you still taste me on your tongue?"

My lips don't move as I remain dumbstruck. His deep chuckle has me flinching. "You look terrified, Little Red. Are you scared someone is going to see me come inside your pretty little pussy?"

I just about shake my head, but he jerks me by my hair, his fingers pinching my scalp, and forces his tongue into my mouth. I melt against him when he groans, willing myself to push him away. The hardness between his legs has me panicking, so my eyes dart toward the door.

"Don't worry, Little Red, it won't take me long to fill you."

My eyes widen when his hand slides up my skirt and his fingers dig into my panties. "So fucking wet for me." He smiles against our kiss.

Then he plunges his fingers in and out of me, and the

sound of my slickness fills the room. Embarrassment creeps over my face at how wet I am for my student.

"Rocco, please." I attempt to push him away, but he stands strong, and when his thumb presses against my aching bud, a rush of arousal spears through me. "Oh god."

"That's it, be a good teacher and coat your student's fingers."

I should be repulsed by his words, but the taboo behind them has me closing my eyes as pleasure consumes me. "That's a greedy girl," he croons in my ear, and my orgasm rips through me.

Rocco

The moment her taut body relaxes, I lift her up onto the desk, push her panties aside, and rush to unbuckle my jeans. She doesn't have time to register me pulling her legs apart before I'm slamming my cock deep inside her.

She's splayed out on her desk like a siren calling to my ferocity. Her mouth opens to scream or resist, but I stuff her fingers between her lips, then plaster my hand over hers, stopping her from removing them as I thrust harder and harder into her.

Her wide eyes are full of fury as the desk moves beneath us.

Then I lean over her, explaining to her how this will play out.

"You're mine, Hallie. All fucking mine."

She attempts to shake her head, but I press against her mouth harder, refusing to let her reject me.

"I own this tight little pussy." I surge inside her with savagery. "Me."

Her whimpers drive me wild, so I drive as deep as humanly possible. "You be a good girl and you get to keep your job." Her chest heaves, and I wish I had more fucking hands to free those tits bursting to get out of her blouse. "Give me what I want, and I'll give you everything. Understand me?"

She whimpers beneath my palm, and I splay out my hand, covering her nose too, and her eyes widen.

"Now, be a good girl and come on my cock. Daddy's missed you so damn much, baby." I deliver a swift thrust for emphasis. "Spray Daddy's cock with your cum, sweet girl." Her eyes flutter, and her pussy tenses around me, forcing my eyes to roll back in ecstasy. After another pump, I come so hard I fall on top of her small form.

We gasp for air, and I finally remove my hand from her mouth.

A sharp crack fills the air, and the sting to my cheek has me rearing back. When I turn to stare into her eyes, the hurt in them has my heart feeling like it's being strangled. Her eyes fill with tears, and her bottom lip trembles.

"I'm sorry. I shouldn't have done that." She blinks and her tears fall, taking with them a piece of me desperate to make amends.

I trail my tongue over her tears, swiping them up as quickly as they fall while I rock my semihard cock in and out of her, hoping to draw out all of my cum.

"It's okay."

"It's not," she whispers. "None of this is okay, Rocco." She pushes against me, but I refuse to move.

The defeat in her tone has my spine straightening.

DECEPTION

Clearly, she hasn't gotten the fucking message.

"I'm not letting you go," I growl as I step back and pull my cock from her. Disappointment ravishes me when my cum drips from her exposed cunt. I hold her legs open with a hand on one knee while I tuck my cock into my pants with the other. Already, the loss of her is creeping in.

"We don't have a choice. You're my student, and I'm your teacher."

I roll my eyes at her.

"Hmm. My teacher with her little cunt dripping with my cum. You're fucking edible, Little Red." I use my thumb to stroke over her slick folds. "Are you going to be good for Daddy while I lick away the excess?"

"Wha-what?"

"I want to taste myself on you." I motion toward her open pussy, and she tries to clamp her legs closed, but I move quicker, using both hands to pry her thighs open.

She glances toward the door. "I have a class soon."

"You better hurry, then." I smirk. "Tell me you're mine and beg Daddy to feed you his cum."

Confusion mars her face as she narrows her eyes. It's adorable to witness.

"I-I ..." She pouts, then twists her lips before shaking her head.

"If you don't beg me, Little Red, your students are going to walk through that door with your needy little cunt exposed while dripping my cum on the floor, and neither one of us wants that."

A whoosh of air leaves her lungs as her cheeks

redden. "Feed me your cum," she grits out, and I raise an eyebrow at her while my fingers dig into her knees. "Please, Daddy. Feed me your cum."

I shake my head. "I don't think so, Little Red. You're being a brat." Her eyes bug out. "Now, tell me you belong to me and ask me nicely to feed you our cum."

She grinds her teeth but the sounds from the other side of the classroom door have her quickly complying.

"Please, Daddy. I'm yours. Please feed me your cum. I'll be your good girl, I promise," her sweet voice delivers, and fuck, if I don't have a choice but to comply this time.

I drop to my knees, and she scrambles onto her elbows to watch me. Our gazes remain locked as I gather up the cum dripping from her pussy with my mouth. "Holy shit," she breathes out, causing my cock to swell with the neediness of her tone.

Then I quickly stand, grab the back of her head, and slam my lips against hers. Our combined cum mingles on her tongue, and while she initially fights me, I ignore her attempts to push my tongue away from hers, and she finally relents.

Her body melts against mine as she sucks the cum from my tongue, and I rejoice in the glory of it.

Our kiss goes from feverish to leisurely, like two lovers finally meeting once again. It's like returning home, and that's what my little red is—home.

I pull back from her lips with reluctance, but I need her to know how I feel. "I'm not going anywhere, Little Red, and neither are you. Nothing and no one will keep you from me. Ever."

Chapter Thirteen

Hallie

Why does the nickname Little Red affect me? The way he delivers it with his filthy tongue wraps around me so possessively my body melts into his with a submission I didn't know I possessed until recently.

Red is considered danger, yet all I feel is safe in his arms.

Red normally means stop, when all I want to do is go.

And red is normally a flag hung as a warning to retreat, and no part of me wants to heed with caution. I only want to throw myself in there and bask in those deterrents.

"I'm not going anywhere, Little Red, and neither are you. Nothing and no one will keep you from me. Ever." His words play out as I tug my laptop bag up on my shoulder.

After swallowing his cum, he allowed me to slip off the desk, and before he left the room, he turned his head over his shoulder and told me not to shower tonight.

As I rush toward my car, all I can think about is doing the opposite of what he asked. The guilt and confusion of having sex with one of my students sends a wave of nausea through me, and I want to wash it away. Even if I like the thought of complying, I've no intentions of doing that.

I can't.

This can't happen.

It can't. No matter how much I crave him.

He's like a drug, and I'm the addict. He's feeding me, fueling my inhibitions with his own, and threatening to ruin everything I've worked so hard to gain.

His warped words of pleasure speak to me on a level I've never known before. Maybe that's it? I've been so used to bland sex that I've clutched onto the first person to offer me a more dangerous and daring experience.

It has to be.

Because Rocco and me cannot happen.

No matter how much I want to bathe in red.

Chapter Fourteen

Rocco

I step off my bike and push it through her gate at the side of her house, then drop the kickstand and dig out her key. It's 2:30 a.m., and after a fucked-up night in one of the clubs, I want nothing more than to see my girl. The woman who grounds me.

Breathing in her scent, I make my way through the kitchen and up the stairs toward her bedroom, taking two steps at a time. The anticipation of seeing her thrums through me like an excitable child eager for more.

I snick open her bedroom door and slip inside, and the warmth of her presence envelops me as I close the door behind me. Adrenaline buzzes through me, so I switch on the small table lamp in the corner of the room, then walk toward the bed and drop my backpack to the floor. I toe off my boots and socks, grab my knife and cell phone from my pocket, and throw my jacket and T-shirt onto the chair I normally watch her from. Then I strip my jeans and boxers down to the floor and kick them aside before crawling onto the bed and over her compliant body.

The sedative I've been giving to her in her nightly smoothies makes her sleep deeply. This normally allows me to watch her while she's unaware, but tonight, it will allow me to spill my seed deep inside her. I part her legs, enjoying the softness of her unmarked skin against my rough hands. My knife glistens in the low lighting, and my cock jumps with anticipation as my mouth literally waters at the prospect of taking her. With a quick slice of my knife, her panties slip free from her, and I discard them to the floor.

Staring down at her pussy, I can already smell her body lotion, and it pisses me off. When I give her instructions not to shower, I expect her to comply.

My teeth ache from gritting them so tightly. She needs to learn who is in charge here and that she doesn't have a choice because her choice is all mine.

As I lower my face to her pussy, annoyance flashes through me. She's washed herself of me, as if trying to eradicate our experience altogether, and frankly, that won't do.

I've waited too long to have her, and now she's trying to get rid of me.

Leaning over her with my phone in hand, I record as I spit on her pussy, once, twice, three times, delighting in

DECEPTION

the spittle dripping from my chin onto her bare cunt. Then I swipe my knife through the pool of spit, ensuring she's coated, and rise up onto my heels and position my cock at her slick entrance. I drop my knife, push one of her knees up to her chest, and hold it in place as I slide my cock inside her painstakingly slowly, determined to make the sensation of taking her last as long as possible. The moment my cock is deep in her cunt, I clench my teeth to fight off the need to unleash on her. She drives me to the point of insanity, and I can't help the need to make her comply, to dominate her and fill her with my child, ensuring our future together.

I film myself as I pull out and surge back inside, deeper, harder, and thrust after thrust becomes feral as my control snaps and I use her little body for my satisfaction. The intense craving I have for her has spiraled, amplifying my obsession with her as sweat coats my skin while my balls ache with desperation. I drop her legs and use my knife to slice through her thin camisole while still continuing to record, and the moment my lips cover her nipple and I suck on the peaked bud, her body reacts. Her pussy contracts, and my mouth falls open in ecstasy as I choke on the strength of my orgasm being ripped from me. "Oh fuck, Little Red." A strangled gasp escapes me as I somehow continue my assault on her little pussy, thrusting my hips to push my cum inside her as deep as humanly possible.

My spent body falls over her, and I quickly roll us so she remains stuffed with my cock but is resting on my chest. With a smug smile, I stroke over her red hair and breathe her in while whispering my promises to keep her.

"You're mine, Little Red. All fucking mine, and I welcome the war we're about to face, because you're worth it."

Chapter Fifteen

Hallie

My fuzzy head takes a moment to come around to the warmth wrapped around my body. Strong arms hold me in place, and somehow, I remain calm as I register just what the hell is happening.

Then a rush of panic hits me as his familiar scent invades my senses, leaving me breathless and aroused.

What the hell is he doing here?

Holy shit, his cock is inside me.

When the hell did this happen?

"Good morning, Hal." His smooth voice has my gaze snapping up toward his as shock lances through me.

"What the hell are you doing?" I attempt to push up from him, but his arms tighten around me, and he chuckles. "Rocco!"

My body betrays me, my core clenching at his controlling behavior.

"Relax." He grins, forcing my mouth to drop open.

Relax?

"It's okay, Little Red."

"O-okay?" I splutter.

"Hm." He strokes my hair, and my body melts under his touch, but I won't allow this to continue. I use this moment to push off him, detaching his cock from me, and fall to the floor.

Rocco shoots up, and I scramble back when I realize I have his cum between my legs. I push aside the thrill of the thought and remain steadfast because this is wrong. So fucking wrong.

"Yo-you came inside me?"

His grin widens, and I can't help but gaze over his naked form. Holy shit, his cock is standing to attention, thick veins running up the side and a pearl of pre-cum dripping from the tip. I squeeze my eyes shut, but snap them open just as quick when he slides to the edge of the bed, towering above me.

"I did." He smirks. "I want to leave a lasting effect on you, and coming inside you is the only way to achieve it, Little Red."

It takes a moment for his words to filter through. The fog of seeing him in his naked glory in my room with his tattoos and abs exposed and his cock jutting upright slows my response. "I-I don't understand." Not at all, but why does the thought heat me inside, and why does my pussy clench, begging for his fullness?

DECEPTION

He chuckles. "Not yet, but you will."

My eyes latch onto my panties on the floor, and I snap my gaze back to his. "We had sex?" I don't know what I'm angrier at, the fact we had sex and he came inside me, or the fact I can't quite remember, even though small snippets trickle in, mainly of him positioning my body and the softness of his lips sucking on my nipple with a contrasting tenderness to his usual wild form. My mouth waters at the thought.

"We did. You said you're mine, and you begged me for it."

My lips move to argue, but I did say I was his, then I remember begging him to stretch me while I was in and out of consciousness.

Holy shit. He's right. I wanted him, and judging by the way my body reacts to his filthy words, I still do.

"You milked my cock dry, like a greedy little slut, Little Red."

My eyes widen. What the hell did he just call me? A slut? However, my pussy seems to like it, because my core clenches and, as if sensing it, Rocco laughs. "You like me degrading you, don't you? It's what helped me fall obsessively in love with you." My mouth falls open, then it drops farther when he jacks his cock in his fist. *In love with me?*

"Come over here and lick your sweet pussy juices from my cock, Little Red. Just like our first time together. Fuck, you've no idea how much I've dreamed about that." He pumps faster. "I couldn't fucking wait to have those lips wrapped around me again, sucking me dry."

My body heats, and I will the floor to open up and swallow me. "Come on. Daddy wants to give you his cum." He bucks, causing my nipples to pebble, and my mouth waters, but the gnawing feeling playing in the back of my mind won't allow me to do as my body so eagerly craves.

He's my student.

He's eighteen.

He says he's in love with me. This is madness, and worse, my body submits to him, craves him even.

"I-I can't."

His gray eyes drill into me with such power and darkness it makes my heart skip a beat. "You want me. I can feel it. You don't have a choice, just like I don't." His eyes hold mine, and a sob catches in my throat because he's right. I don't have a choice; I want him, even though I shouldn't.

My mind is at war with my body, but in Rocco's proximity, I've never felt so alive. He has all the control, and I simply comply.

"Now, crawl over here and do as you're fucking told. I already have to punish you for your insolence." I remain frozen to the spot, utter shock leaving me unable to function. "Do you want the faculty knowing you fuck your students?" Tears fill my eyes, and I shake my head. "Now, crawl over here and do as you're fucking told, Little Red. You're pissing me off, and I want to come. But I need to punish you first."

I jolt and narrow my eyes, causing him to chuckle maniacally. "What? You thought I'd let the fact you tried

DECEPTION

to wash me from you slide?" I shake my head, unable to find the words to argue with him. I never imagined he would be in my home, let alone waking up to his cock stuffed inside me. The fact he used me while I slept should make feel repulsed and violated, not turned on.

It's some sort of midlife crisis, it has to be.

"Crawl," he barks, then points toward his feet. "Be my good little slut and do as I ask, and I won't make you suffer too long." He raises his eyebrow, and I swallow back the fear of his threat and raise up on all fours, giving in to the dull ache to become submissive to him. "Good," he croons as I move. His fist works faster, causing pre-cum to drip from the tip and slide down his tattooed fingers, and my body preens in delight at the way he reacts to me.

Stopping at his feet, I raise my eyes to meet his dark ones glaring down at me. The lust oozing from him penetrates the walls of anger I've built and fills the cavern with desire as every red flag he holds slips from my mind.

I've never crawled for a man in my entire life. I've never been spoken to in a sexual way like this either, but the possessiveness behind his words has me submitting.

"Now, lick my fingers clean."

When I lean forward, his hand remains locked around his cock, and his knuckles whiten as I swipe my tongue over his digits. "Fuck," he says through clenched teeth as he thrusts up. "Jesus, Hal." As I obey, his tone is full of awe, and gone is the man who was threatening me only moments ago. One of his hands finds my hair, tangling in the curls to the point of pain while the other continues to jerk himself off. "Over the tip, watch me spill for you, and fucking clean it up," he grits out, and the muscles on his neck protrude as I lick the swollen head.

His cock leaks, and I moan when I suck the tip into my mouth. Swiping the pre-cum from his slit has his abs contracting beneath me. "Fuck me, you can be a good girl, Hal." *Thrust.* "You can be my good slut." His cock hits the back of my mouth before he withdraws. "You can be a good girl for your daddy." *Thrust.* My pussy becomes wet with need. "You can fucking obey when you need to." *Thrust.* He wrenches my head back, and I gasp for air. He lifts his ass from the bed and jerks his cock with fervor above my face, causing shameless arousal to slip between my legs. Warm cum splashes my cheeks, lips, and chin, coating me in his pleasure. "Fuckkk," he roars into the room while I sag against his restraint.

Chest heaving, he comes down from his orgasm, and his glazed eyes become focused, then his lips tip into a smirk.

"Now it's time for your punishment."

Chapter Sixteen

Hallie

"Now it's time for your punishment." My blood runs cold at the darkness in his voice. "Shh, don't worry, Little Red. I'd never hurt you," he whispers, dragging the pad of his thumb down my cheek while scooping up some of his cum to rub across my bottom lip. "I'm kind of angry you made me lose control; I want all my cum inside your pussy so you can get pregnant as soon as possible."

His words are like a bucket of icy water being thrown over me, washing me of any arousal as his intentions sink in.

He stands and moves around me while I remain stunned in a heap on the floor. "You can't be serious?" I finally spit out.

"Deadly," he throws over his shoulder as he opens a backpack on the floor.

"Pregnant? Rocco, whatever is happening here is not long term. It's to stop you from—" He places a finger over my mouth. The smell of his cum and the way his wayward hair falls into his eyes have me itching to touch him with the affection of a partner, and that's absurd, given the circumstances, but something about him has me willingly drowning in this unhealthy obsession.

"Shh, don't piss me off any more than you already have. I don't want you to hate me." Then he pulls back and allows some thick synthetic rope to slip through his fingers until it hits the floor. "On the bed."

I dart my eyes toward the clock, knowing I don't have time to play whatever game this is. "Rocco, I ..." I shake my head.

"You're not going to work, and I'm not going to class. I've already sent the messages to school."

My eyes widen. "What?"

He smiles, as if proud of himself. "I'm going to spend the day punishing you, filling you with my cum, and reminding you of our future together." His gaze latches onto my stomach, and I cover myself with my hands. This only turns his gaze more furious than earlier, and I swallow back the lump forming in my throat.

"This is fucked up," I whisper, but my blood pumps with arousal.

Why does everything so bad feel so good?

"You're right, Little Red. It is fucked up. Our fucked up. Now get on the bed before I fuck you up so bad you won't be able to walk into school tomorrow either. You don't want to have to explain to the principal why, now, do you?"

A fresh tear falls down my face, and I shake my head. His expression softens but quickly disappears. "On the bed, Hallie."

Rocco

I sit in the chair and take a sip of my water while Hallie struggles against the bindings again. Seeing her ball tied for me has my cock pleading for gratification once again, despite taking her dozens of times already. It's as if I have an endless supply of cum solely for her.

She's on her side, with my cum coating her pussy lips. Her eyes implore mine, filled with tears due to the edging I've been using to punish her.

Her mouth is bound by the rope, and I'm certain she will have marks on her tender skin that will need to be treated when I release her.

The buzz of her phone has me shooting up from my chair. As I stare down at the name, I press decline and decide to let her deal with that later, assuming she can be a good girl for me from now on.

I pick up my treasured knife and make my way around the bed, watching in fascination as her pupils dilate when they latch onto my hand. It's not in fear—I could sense that; I'm used to fear. No, my little red is intrigued.

Slowly, I bring the knife to the corner of her mouth and slice through the ropes, and she spits them out quickly. "Thank you."

"Good girl." I glide the blade over her skin, down her neck, causing goose bumps to trail over her. Then I circle her nipple with the tip, flicking it with a well-practiced technique learned by years of training before continuing down to my little red's swollen cunt. I spin the knife so the blade is in the palm of my hand and slide the hilt inside her while pressing my thumb to her little clit. "Don't come," I warn, and she gifts me with a compliant nod. One that has been very absent until now. "Fuck yourself on it."

Her breath hitches, and I glare at her, then her body falls lax, and she moves her hips, taking the knife handle like a good submissive.

My eyes never leave her cunt as I add pressure to her clit. "Do you want to come?"

"Please."

"Please what?"

I flick my gaze up to hers as I stop my thumb from moving. Once again edging her. "Please what, Little Red?"

She licks her lips, and her eyes plead with me to show her compassion, to give her what I've stolen all day long, but she needs to learn who is in charge, who owns this hot little body now. "Please, Daddy. I want to come."

"And?" I grind out.

DECEPTION

"And I want your cum deep inside me, Daddy."

Fuck me, hearing her say those words is like liquid gold.

"And?"

"I want you to put a baby in me."

My cock spurts on her words, and I withdraw the knife in a flash. Her body slumps, but I don't have time to reassure her. Instead, I mount her, positioning myself with one knee on the mattress and my leg over her tied legs. Then I slam my cock into her so hard she stills.

"There you go. Good fucking girl. Now, come on Daddy's cock, Little Red."

As her pussy convulses, I rock my hips. "Oh god, Rocco, holy " To heighten her orgasm, I thrust my thumb into her ass, and she thrashes from side to side. My cock, once again, spurts with unadulterated pleasure.

I lean over her ear. "Good girls get fucked. Bad girls get fucked over. Remember that, Little Red."

Chapter Seventeen

Hallie

After fucking me into oblivion, Rocco carried me into the shower, then placed me on the bench and got down on his knees to wash me, taking extra care and attention around the marks on my wrist and ankles.

Being tied up was another new experience for me, and, again, not one I disapprove of, no matter how much I fought him. The man withheld my orgasms, playing my body against itself until he got what he wanted—my compliance.

I lie on his chest, listening to the steady beat of his heart while he plays with my hair. How can I be so relaxed and calm when I know how deranged the man lying beneath me is?

Yet something inside me calls to him. His brokenness

and obsession don't scare me as they probably should, they only excite me.

Maybe my dull previous marriage caused me to become so reckless, to seek excitement from someone else, something I never had before, or felt.

"I can hear you thinking," he whispers against my head, placing a tender kiss there.

I smile against this chest. "Really? I doubt that."

"You're thinking about how good we are together."

A strangled choke leaves me. He's being serious, and when I turn my head to face him, I see the sincerity as clear as day. *Oh, sweet Jesus, I'm totally screwed. My life will be over. My career in shambles, and my family will disown me.*

He tenses below me. "I admit, I'm not entirely sure what you're thinking right now, but I need you to stop it before you piss me off."

His words have me wanting to soothe him, to replace his anger with the softness he hides, so I lick my lips and slowly move my hand toward his cheek, relishing the way he turns into my touch. I caress his handsome face and over his jaw while his hand moves down my spine and over my ass. "I can't wait to fuck your ass, Hal. Your tight little ass sucked my thumb in so well." My breath hitches. How can he be so sweet and crude at the same time? "Have you been fucked here before, Little Red?" He squeezes my ass cheek hard, then palms it gently, taking away the bite of pain.

My face burns under his scrutiny. "No."

A wicked grin spreads over his face. "Good. I didn't

think so, but knowing my cock is going to break your tight hole open makes me very happy."

My face reddens.

He slaps my ass hard. "Not yet, though. I want my baby inside you first."

"Rocco ..." I try to reason, but he shakes his head, as if warning me to stop speaking, and my body sags.

In all honesty, it doesn't matter that he comes inside me as long as he's clean. When I first slept with him, I made a trip to the pharmacy, and they gave me Plan B and the pill just in case I wanted to take it too.

He slides from beneath me, and his solid ass tightens as he strides toward his jeans and pulls them on. "I'm going to go and make us some food. You haven't eaten all day, and I don't like the thought of you and my baby hungry." He winks at me before heading toward the door while I throw a hand over my face and fall back into the pillow. His words sink in, bringing with them a wave of nausea. I know deep in my soul that he has no intentions of letting me go and, worse, I don't want him to.

Whatever crazy train this is, we're on it together, and I'm not ready to get off.

I don't know if I ever will be, and that thought unnerves me the most. If my ex-husband finds out about Rocco, he will go insane, and knowing what power he holds over both me and the city causes a rush of panic to slice through me.

This needs to stop.

I pick up my phone, and my stomach sinks at my

missed calls, but instead of dealing with them, I open my messages to Sharna.

> Me: Guess who walked into class yesterday?

> Sharna: (Shrug emoji)

> Me: Rocco.

> Sharna: The toyboy.

I wince at her choice of words.

> Me: Yes.

> Sharna: Holy shit, Hal. What are you going to do?

> Me: He's kind of blackmailing me.

> Sharna: No way.

> Me: Yes. He told me I'm his.

> Sharna: No way.

> Sharna: You want him though, right?

Ugh, why can't she be the adult and tell me what we're doing is wrong.

> Sharna: You deserve to have fun.

DECEPTION

Me: Did you miss the part where I said he's blackmailing me?

Sharna: You should thank him. You want him.

Sharna: Admit it.

Me: I do. But I shouldn't.

Sharna: (Eye roll emoji).

Me: He's here. In my house. Cooking for me.

Sharna: Are you kidding?

Sharna: Is he naked?

I choke on a laugh. Trust her to not see the severity of the situation.

Me: Please be serious, Sharn. What am I going to do?

Sharna: Can you report him?

A ball of dread fills my stomach as I bite into my lip and contemplate my next move. But ultimately, I don't want to. There's far too much at stake.

Me: No.

BJ ALPHA

> Sharna: Then let him fuck you senseless until he gets you out of his system.

I scoff at her words as they filter through me. Something tells me Rocco is sticking around and I'm totally screwed. Instead of panicking at the prospect, I feel excitement.

Chapter Eighteen

Rocco

I throw in some sliced peppers and another dash of soy sauce, and the moment she enters the kitchen, I'm aware. Call it a sixth sense, if you will, but I feel her in my bones, and my body relaxes at her closeness.

"How did you know I liked stir fry?" she quizzes from the doorway, looking like a little siren in my T-shirt. It makes me want to beat my fists on my chest like a neanderthal and shout she's mine and I'll kill anyone who dares to look at her.

"It's your refrigerator." I point toward it. "Figured you liked what's in there." My lip quirks up. "Besides, I know more about you than you think." I stir the vegetables as her gaze roams over me. I'm muscled, tattooed, young, and hot as fuck in that bad boy way women love, so I'm confident in my body, especially while knowing

I'm the opposite of her ex and how wet her pussy gets for me.

Hallie took a walk on the wild side, and now she's so addicted she can barely walk. I smirk at my analogy.

"Like what?"

I turn the heat down and give the vegetables another stir. Striding toward her, I lift her up by her hips, causing her to squeal until I drop her ass on the counter and step between her legs. Then I lift my T-shirt up to her neck. "Like how you come so easily when I play with your nipples." I suck one into my mouth, and her fingers thread through my hair, holding me in place while her spine arches as I gently lick over the tip, loving the way it peaks. I palm her tits, pushing them together. My cock hardens at the heavy weight in my hands, and I want to roar with possession at the sensation.

"Oh god."

I stop sucking and glance up at her in warning, and she gazes down at me, stealing my breath, but I refuse to back down. She needs to learn what I want from her and obey.

It's adorable when heat colors her face while I wait for her compliance. "Please, Daddy. Lick my nipple."

My hips buck involuntarily. "Fuck," I pant as I go back to licking over the hardened bud.

"More. I want you to suck it too."

Fucking Jesus, yes. That's what I'm talking about.

Her ass shifts forward when I wrap my lips around her nipple and gently suck.

DECEPTION

"This okay? Or do you want harder?" My cock leaks against my jeans.

"Just like that." She likes my tenderness against her nipple, a contrast to my usual brutish self, and I like it too.

She bucks again. "Fuck. Can you orgasm like this?" I watch her from beneath my hooded eyes the lust in my own mirroring hers.

"I-I don't know, I think so."

Knowing she's never orgasmed from nipple stimulation is like an aphrodisiac, and the way her nails claw at my scalp, giving away her need, has me eager to please her.

"I'mmm ..." She throws her head back, and I stare up at her as she unravels in my arms from the use of my tongue against her tits.

"Fuck," I breathe out as my cock spits pre-cum, eager to get in on the action.

My phone rings, and I grumble at knowing my absence is no longer going unnoticed.

Hallie stills above me while I reluctantly release her nipple and step away from her, hating the loss of her touch.

Picking up my phone, I bring it to my ear. "Where the fuck have you been?"

I drag a hand through my hair at the sound of my brother's furious voice.

"You know what, don't fucking answer that. I know exactly where you fucking are. Where you are every damn night."

I tug on my hair, feeling myself spiral, and walk

toward the back door while watching Hallie in the reflection of the window move over toward the stove. "It'll serve you well to remember that," he snaps.

A red haze comes over me at my brother's insinuation. "Don't fucking threaten me, Rafael," I grit out through clenched teeth, my tone just as low and deadly.

He huffs, undeterred by my threat.

"Get your ass back home. I expect you there in fifteen minutes, otherwise I'll inform Papa of your little deception," he spits out with spite, and my spine snaps straight.

"Fuck you." I end the call, but we both know I will be there; I've no choice. Not yet anyway.

"Is everything okay?"

Her sweet voice wraps around me, and as I turn to face her, my heart seizes. Fuck me, she's so damn beautiful.

So fucking beautiful it hurts. I rub at the pain in my chest as I take in her small stature and wild red curls. The way she nibbles on her bottom lip as she waits for me to answer has me itching to tug it into my mouth.

"I need to go," I state, unable to say home, not when my home is with her. It has been for the last two years, however unaware she's been.

Her shoulders droop, and she stares down at her bare feet, and I hate the disappointment that's washed over her. Stepping forward, I lift her chin with my finger, forcing her to face me. "I'll see you in class tomorrow."

"Rocco, we can't—"

I silence her with my finger to her lips. "Shhh."

She shakes her head, but I remain steadfast.

"We are."

"If I get found out." Fear swims in her eyes, and I hate it. The thought has me going over my plan in my mind. I need to speed things up, and that starts with ensuring she's mine and getting rid of this charade of a wedding my father believes will happen.

"We won't get found out, and you wouldn't take the fall for it even if we did."

Her eyes search my face. "What does that even mean?"

"It means I'd take the blame in whatever shape or form I'd need to, Little Red."

Her lips part on a gasp, and I slide my finger into her mouth.

"I'll always protect you as long as you remain mine." I gift her forehead with a kiss, then pull back, hating the way my cock weeps without satisfaction only she can bring.

"I'll go grab my boots and backpack, then head out."

"Okay," she whispers as I head toward the door leading to the stairs.

"And Hallie?"

"Mmm?"

"Wear something sexy to class." I wink, causing a blush to break out over her freckled cheeks.

Chapter Nineteen

Hallie

A slow smile spreads over my face as I glance over my shoulder with a confidence normally absent from me. I feel sexy and professional all in one. The garters are hidden beneath my pencil skirt, and they're not something I would normally wear, but one night over the course of my divorce, Sharna and I spent an evening drinking cheap wine, and I ordered a pile of clothes that Gerrard would have forbid me to wear. She said I deserved it, and I couldn't agree more. I'd spent years being suppressed and was ready to simply be me.

Since Rocco left last night, I haven't stopped thinking about the way my body lights up beneath his touch. His degrading words wrap around me and bring me a sense of warmth I've never experienced, a need I've never encountered, and a craving I never knew I wanted.

I glance at my phone and swipe the latest message from Gerrard off the screen. I can't deal with him, not when I have to endure his presence this weekend, so instead, I shove my phone in my laptop bag and head toward the door.

After my meeting with the principal to discuss my absence yesterday, my morning ran slow. At lunch, I searched the cafeteria for Rocco, to no avail. I might have felt his eyes on me, but I never saw him, making me wonder if I was paranoid.

So, when the class period begins, a pang of nervousness fills me. I want to see him, but then I worry about how I will react. Will people look at us and know what we've done?

What if he doesn't look at me the same way? With the heated gaze that sets my body alight.

I chew on my bottom lip, ignoring the hustle and bustle of the classroom while everyone takes a seat.

"You okay?" I snap my eyes up at the sound of his velvety tone as he leans over my desk, and I take a deep breath, inhaling his cologne, and my mouth waters.

Jesus, he's gorgeous.

I close my eyes momentarily, once again kicking myself for falling for a student. An eighteen-year-old student.

When I open my eyes, his narrowed gaze roams over my face, and I soften at the concern marring his.

"I'm fine...now," I tack on, and his coiled muscles relax. A smile plays on his lips, then he nods and turns to walk toward his desk.

"Looks like the new kid has a stiffy for Ms. Davis too, huh?" Blair, one of the jocks, jokes, and I cringe at the implication.

Rocco flies through the air so quick I barely have time to blink. He grabs Blair by the scruff of his neck. "What the fuck did you just say?"

I rush toward them while two of Blair's friends attempt to pull Rocco away, but his grip tightens, causing Blair to become red-faced and his eyeballs bulge.

"Rocco! Stop, right now!" I scream as I rush over to them.

Ignoring me as the veins on his temple protrude, his grip tightens on Blair's neck. "I'm warning you, Rocco!" I bellow.

He turns his face to glare at me. "Warning me?" He lifts a brow, making me swallow at the threat behind it.

"Ye-yes. Warning you." My voice quivers, and I hate it.

As if sensing my discomfort, Rocco releases Blair and pushes him back into his chair. "Next time, I'll take it out on your mouth, motherfucker."

Blair sucks in sharp gulps of air while rubbing his throat.

Maybe I should send him to the emergency room? Nausea swirls in my stomach at the thought. "Dick," Blair mumbles, and I decide against it.

Grumbles and whines come from the students as Rocco throws himself into his chair with a heavy huff.

"Any more outbursts, and you'll all be sent to the principal," I spit out to no one in particular as I stride toward my desk, ignoring the startled gasps of the class.

This is going to be one hell of a lesson.

Rocco

"Any more outbursts, and you'll all be sent to the principal." Her sweet ass sways as she makes her way toward the front of the class, and not for the first time, I scan her delectable body from top to toe. My blood pumps with a need to mark her as mine. To have every fucker know she belongs to me.

Turning my attention away from her, I send the little punk who dared to insinuate shit between me and my girl a death glare, and he darts his eyes away like the coward he is.

I might only have been at this school a few days, but my reputation precedes me. Since the first time I came to Matt's rescue, people know who I am, and I find it somewhat amusing that the girl who has me all wrapped up doesn't.

She will soon.

Very fucking soon.

The bell rings, and I haven't so much as lifted my

pen. How the fuck can I when all I can think about is her sweet pussy clenching my fingers or the way her snug cunt pulled the handle of my knife inside her, covering it in her cum while she rode it so beautifully.

The room empties, and finally, I'm alone with her.

I watch in sick satisfaction as her fingers tremble against the wood of her desk.

My poor little red is nervous. I lick my lips, the predator in me roaring to be released like a caged animal.

"Lock the door." I tilt my head toward the door, and she follows my action before obeying. Then she turns to face me, her back against the door, her chest heaving, and no doubt, her pussy is dripping too.

Pushing back in my chair, I stalk toward her. My eyes never leave hers, and when I finally reach her, I wrap my fingers in her curls, pulling her toward me and forcing our mouths to collide.

Our kiss is hungry, feverish, and full of passion. It's everything.

I slide my hand up her skirt and still at the lace of her garters. A flash of pain hits my balls, and my mouth becomes dry at knowing she obeyed so submissively. "Good girl."

Her breath hitches, and I slam my lips against hers to devour her once again.

Her hands find my jeans button, and she pops it open, scrambling to free my cock while I push her skirt up her thighs and slide her panties to the side. When her hand wraps around my cock, I swear I see stars. Her touch is worth the world, and I'm the center of it.

DECEPTION

I lift her up against the door, and she lines me up, then I power into her, forcing her teeth to bite into my neck to withhold the scream she wants to let out.

Fuck, I love knowing she's marked me, and with that thought, I lift my T-shirt over my head with her assistance, then drop it to the floor. "Again. Bite me again," I grit out.

Her pussy clenches around me, and her nails dig into my shoulders as she pulls me toward her. Then she sinks her teeth into the muscle of my shoulders, following it up with a soothing swipe of her tongue that makes my hips stutter. "Oh, fuck, Little Red, you feel so good."

She moans at my words, and I will her to tell me what I want to hear.

"I want you." She licks my neck. "I shouldn't, but I do."

I ram into her harder, each admittance driving us higher and higher as her teeth and lips devour my flesh.

"I want to call you Daddy."

"Fuckkk," I choke out as my balls draw up. "More," I growl, knowing I'm almost fucking there, but not wanting to be.

"I want to feel your cum inside me."

My eyes roll back. "Yes. Fuck, yes. My good little slut."

"Yes. Like Daddy's good slut, I want it leaking out of me."

Sweat drips from my forehead. "Holy fuck, Little Red," I grunt. "Tell Daddy you're his little slut. Tell me you're mine."

"I'm yours." Her pussy clenches, and my cock erupts as her teeth snag my skin, sending a wave of pleasure through me while her pussy milks me dry with the impact of her orgasm.

"I want you, Rocco," she whispers. "I shouldn't, but I do, and it terrifies me."

"Don't be scared, I've got you, Little Red. I'll always catch you when you fall." I lift my eyes to implore hers, but we're cut off when the door handle jiggles and voices filter through, causing us both to still.

"Can you believe that prick? He thinks he can touch me. All because the teacher is a cock tease."

Hallie stiffens beneath me, and I grind my teeth as we remain frozen, listening to the conversation playing out.

"Leave it alone, man," his buddy begs, and I scramble to recognize his voice. Darryl Davis, Gerrard's nephew.

"No chance. He doesn't come into my school and think he can overthrow me, and the cock tease is going down too." He laughs. His friend doesn't respond, and fortunately for him, it saved him from my wrath.

He might not realize it yet, but this Blair prick has sealed his fate.

Nobody calls my girl a cock tease and gets away with it.

Nobody.

Chapter Twenty

Rocco

Her cheeks glow the most gorgeous shade of red when she sees what I have laid out on the bed for her.

"Wh-what is that?"

I step up behind her and place my arm across her chest, holding her by her throat. "That's so I can watch our baby being created." I push the red waves of hair off her shoulder with my nose and place a kiss against her neck. Her pulse skitters beneath my touch, and I relish it.

Her chest heaves, pushing those glorious tits of her against my hold. "I-I don't understand."

"It's okay, Little Red. Daddy is going to show you."

I release her, and her body droops. I'm unsure if it's from disappointment or relief, but in all honesty, I don't care. She will beg for my touch soon enough.

"Take your clothes off and get on the bed. I want you

on all fours". Her breath hitches, and she spins to face me. While holding my gaze with an air of confidence, she slowly undresses, dropping one item after the other while my mouth waters and my eyes eat up her movements like a predator.

Once she's naked, she spins on the balls of her feet and flicks her hair over her shoulder, then saunters over to the bed, and my cock jumps at the way her luscious ass sways as she does.

Languidly, she climbs on the bed, giving me a show that has my body wrung taut with anticipation. Fuck me, she's a goddess, a red siren calling to my demonic self. The perfect woman—a combination of fire and spirit, with the precise blend of submissiveness to balance her inner desires.

The room fills with a sexual tension—an awareness of fire simmering between, desperate to burst into robust flames.

I lift my T-shirt over my head, and pride forces my chest to swell at the way her eyes flare with lust, then I toe off my boots and socks. Staring back at her heated face, I drop my jeans and kick them to the side. She licks her lips, and my cock jumps and pre-cum falls from the tip in a long stream of eagerness.

My gaze latches onto the tools on the bed, and I clear my throat, determined to keep on track with my plan—watch myself impregnate her.

Moving behind her, I pick up the remote and put the television on. The screen is blank, for now, but not for long.

DECEPTION

"Watch the television. Eyes ahead," I purr as I slide my palm down her spine and grip her ass cheek, loving the fullness of it in my hand. "So fucking hot." I slap it hard, and she turns her head over her shoulder to face me. "I said, eyes ahead." I slap her harder this time, and she quickly averts her gaze. "Good girl, Little Red." My smooth voice has her pushing her ass cheek into my open hand, and I chuckle at her need for praise.

Then I bend and spit on my cock before repeating the action on her ass.

"Oh god." She lifts her hips as I drag my cock from her ass to slit, spreading my spittle on her.

Pressing record on the television remote. I smile to myself. This may be the moment our baby is conceived, and we will spend every damn day rewatching it if we want to. I pick up the camera tube and lube it. Then, with two fingers, I open my girl's wet pussy. "Let Daddy inside, pretty girl," I croon as I slide the small device inside her slick pussy. "Let me watch inside you." The screen fills with her slick pink pussy, and my balls ache, so I've no choice but to pinch the tip of my cock to stop myself from coming.

"Holy shit!" She gasps as she stares straight ahead. I take this moment to line the head of my dripping cock up and slowly slide inside her. "Oh wow. Oh, Jesus."

"Fuck." My mouth falls open when the head of my cock becomes visible on the screen.

The possession flowing through my bloodstream is pure indescribable euphoria as I take a hold of her hips and repeat the action of sliding in and out of her. My mouth becomes dry and need zips up my spine.

"Do you see? Do you see Daddy fucking this little pussy, owning it?" I slap her ass for emphasis, and she clenches around me. The action captured on screen gives me no choice but to move faster. Her pussy becomes wetter and wetter, coating my cock in her juices with each clench of her muscles, and it's hot as fuck.

"Daddy's going to put his baby right here." I slam inside her, loving the feeling and vision of my cock rubbing on her internal walls. "Daddy's going to give you his seed."

"Yes."

I slam harder into her.

"Please, Daddy."

"Be a good girl and watch me fuck my baby into you, Little Red."

My hips work faster, my cock sinking deeper.

"Yes, Daddy. Please."

Electricity ignites my body, every cell alive with pure unadulterated bliss as I fuck my cock deeper and deeper into her wet pussy.

As my feral need builds, I take a hold of her hair in my fist and yank her head upright. "Look! Look at Daddy filling you with his baby."

A gasp leaves her lips as she takes in the scene of my cock stroking her inner walls.

"P-please," she snivels out, the desperation in her sweet voice catalytic.

DECEPTION

"Watch Daddy fill you with his cum." She pushes against me with a guttural moan.

I clench my teeth and keep my eyes ahead, desperate to see my cum enter her despite the need to slam my eyes shut as the pressure builds.

My balls pull up tight, and I've no choice but to slam deeper, forcing the slit of my cock to open as lashes of my warm cum flood her pussy. Power surges through me at the sight. Thick white cum coats her slick walls, and her pussy convulses, milking me of my seed.

"Look at Daddy's cum making you pregnant, Little Red." The words spill from me in awe.

"Ohh ..." Her pussy continues to squeeze me, and I want to spank her ass for it as well as pleasure her. The sight on screen is like nothing I've ever witnessed.

Watching our cum blend deep inside her is pure, unhinged beauty.

It may well be the moment my girl gets pregnant, and I intend to watch it over and over again while I lick her clean, refill her, and repeat every action in every position possible. "My girl deserves my babies, don't you, Little Red?"

"Yes, Daddy." Her compliance is my undoing, and I lose my balance and fall onto her back, slamming us both onto the mattress while keeping her plugged with my cock to enable my cum to remain secure inside her.

Just where it belongs.

Chapter Twenty-One

Rocco

I drop the kickstand and peer up at the mansion before me, and with a low whistle, I take it in. Everything about it screams money, but it doesn't scream power. If it did, there would be cameras on every corner, security on the gates, and bodyguards keeping little Blair Hardwick in check. Instead, the heir to the Hardwick Legal Dynasty has none of it.

The dumbasses think living in an influential area where crime is merely in the underbelly of society keeps them safe from harm's way.

Wrong.

So fucking wrong.

Call the wrong man's girl a cock tease, and nothing will keep you safe. Not even daddy's money.

Especially from a monster. A man like me born and

bred in the very underbelly of modern society while maintaining the dignified silence their society insists on. I'm the boogeyman in the shadows, the orchestrator of nightmares, and tonight, Blair Hardwick will never speak a bad word again.

He will face fears he never knew he had.

A rush of exhilaration floods my entire body as I climb the wall with ease and drop down onto the ground with a huff. Then I saunter across the well-manicured lawns and head straight toward the French doors. The fancy doors are no deterrent as I take my knife from my shoulder holster and flick it open. I have an array of toys to play with tonight, but this one is by far my favorite, especially knowing Hallie comes on it like a geyser.

I use the knife to pry the door open with well-practiced ease. Then I push into the office, listening for any clue that I might have disturbed the Hardwick family.

Nothing.

When I asked Silas to check over the floor plans, he delivered me with the exact route I need to take to get to the prick's bedroom. As I make my way toward the back staircase, I do so while knowing this entire wing is his, but tonight, it's my playing field to deliver justice.

Slowly, I turn the handle to his bedroom door and step inside. Every cell in my body is alive with adrenaline. This is what I do best, what I've been trained to do, and like the deranged man I am, I fucking love it.

He's snoring in his bed, laid out like a starfish on his back, and my lip quirks at how easy he's made it for me.

DECEPTION

From my holster, I withdraw a set of ropes and tape. Using a technique my father taught me, I create two loops and loosely drape them over his feet and the bedpost. The moment he moves, they will tighten like a snare. Then I repeat the action with his wrists, loosely binding them, ready for his fight.

His breathing changes, as if finally recognizing something touching him, but he drifts back into the deep sleep and loud snores fill the room.

I tilt my head as I analyze him and can't help but wonder if he will make the same noise when he no longer has his tongue?

Rolling out the tape, I rip a piece off and, in a flash, I slap it over his mouth. His eyes dart open as he thrashes about on the bed like a fish out of water. I laugh maniacally at my thoughts, then switch on the lamp beside his bed. His eyes widen as they take me in, and his chest rises and falls in panic.

"That's right, little Blair boy, it's the new kid who needs to learn his place." I walk around the bed and tighten the restraints, loving that he attempts to lash out but remains incapacitated. I chuckle when he exhales through his nostrils and his face reddens. "Oh, and let's not forget the way you called Ms. Davis a cock tease." Using her surname feels like acid on my tongue, and I withdraw my knife, reveling in the way it brings me comfort and him fear.

With his eyes locked on mine, I slide the blade into my mouth, licking the coldness of it. Pressing it deeper, adrenaline flashes through me when copper hits my tastebuds, and even better, I swear I can still taste the tang of her sweet pussy as I work my tongue down the handle. Swiping my blood across my cheek, I smirk down at him.

He sobs and thrashes about while I shrug off my jacket, coolly placing it on his study chair, then I climb onto the bed and straddle his broad chest. He's a quarterback, so he's broad, and in that moment, I'm half tempted to maim him enough to destroy his career too.

The guy looks fit to explode. Every vein pulsates on his face, protruding so perfectly that if my knife pierced just one of them, I could create the perfect canvas of retribution with his blood.

I drag the tip of the blade down his face, sliding it through the sweat now coating his skin. "You shouldn't have called her anything bad, Blair." He sniffles as sweat beads down his face. "I warned you, but you didn't listen." A sob catches in his throat as he bucks up in a lame attempt to throw me off him. "Now you've left me no choice but to make sure you never speak a bad word about her again. Do you understand?"

He nods, with a muffled sound behind his gag.

"I'm not sure you do." I tilt my head to the side.

He protests behind the tape as my knife digs into his chin, forcing his head up and exposing those glorious juicy veins on his neck. I lick my lips and try to stay on target.

My plan is to incapacitate the kid, not kill him. Not unless absolutely necessary, anyway.

"When I leave this room, you so much as acknowledge her or mention me being here, and I will cut off your cock. Do you understand?"

A strangled noise leaves his throat.

"Good. Now it's time for me to ensure you never speak badly again. Take your punishment like a man, and I'll be done with you. Understand?"

Tears fill his eyes, and I withdraw my knife to give him the opportunity to nod, which he does. The stench of piss filling the room only adds to my heightened state. I've become accustomed to the way a victim begs, and it only gets my cock hard. Until now, I never had a way to satiate it, but knowing I can sink into my girl when I leave here has me slicing through the center of the tape.

I push my fingers into his cheeks before he has time to speak, forcing his tongue from his mouth and offering it to me on a silver platter.

A heavy cry has me taking pity on him. Where I'd normally drag the punishment out to inflict the most pain possible, I decide to handle Blair's punishment quickly. Besides, the sooner I get this over with, the quicker I can get back and fill her with my cum.

I slice through his organ, and his eyes bulge as blood spurts out of his mouth and he chokes, spluttering the mess over his bed sheets. Happy with the knowledge he won't so much as utter another word, I slide off the bed, then tuck my knife away. I grab my jacket and slip it on, then head toward the door, unable to stop myself from whistling with the buzz of the adrenaline ravishing my veins, making me appear all the more crazed.

With my hand on the door handle, I glance over my

shoulder. "Don't forget, Blair. I can make this a whole lot worse."

He nods profusely as I step through the door safe with the knowledge the kid won't breathe a damn word, and he sure as shit won't be saying it either.

Chapter Twenty-Two

Hallie

It's been four nights since Rocco slid inside my bed smelling of blood. He chuckled when I mentioned it and asked how I knew what blood smelled like. When I told him my ex was a police officer and I've had my fair share of enduring the aftermath of his violent shifts, something changed inside him.

He's always volatile and rough when we have sex, but I'm sure the mention of my ex riled him even further. The soreness is heavy between my legs after he slammed inside me so hard the headboard came apart, and still, he didn't stop. The sheer lustful anger and determination on his face as he powered inside me has me squeezing my legs together as I smooth out my red dress.

Meeting my ex for dinner is not how I like to spend every first Sunday of the month, but it's something I agreed to, to keep the peace. I forgo any makeup, only applying lip gloss, and don't even spritz my perfume because I refuse to have him acknowledge it. Any way I can divert his attention from me and onto why we're meeting, I will do.

Because that's why I'm doing this.

My family is everything to me.

And Rocco is quickly becoming a part of that.

Rocco

"How often do you have to do this again?" I glance toward Matt as he drives us toward his house.

"Once a month. My parents agreed to it. It's meant to create a united front for the family."

I scoff at his words.

"Right?" He shakes his head. "I don't get it either." Then he drags his hand through his hair. "It's just another excuse for my dad to try to control my mom."

I sit forward at his comment. "What do you mean?"

He chuckles, but it lacks humor. "I'm not dumb enough to know my dad fought so hard for custody of me to punish my mom."

"For leaving him?"

He swallows hard. "Yeah. He thought she'd stay."

"Do you wish she had?" I quiz.

"Fuck no. She deserves better. That's why I said I wanted to stay with my dad." He shrugs.

My gaze travels over his face, and I can tell he's

holding back, but I don't want to push him, not with knowing what's about to come.

"Your dad was okay with you bringing me to dinner?" I ask.

He shrugs a shoulder. "I asked if I could bring a friend over, and he swatted me away like a bug. It's not like he's ever asked about my friends." His solemn voice makes my heart constrict, which is weird because I often question if I have a heart at all.

Yet Hallie and Matt bring something out in me; it's both terrifying and freeing.

I slap Matt's shoulder. "Well, don't worry, buddy. I'm the best friend anyone could ever wish for. What more could a man ask?"

He snorts. "You'd be surprised, and don't take this the wrong way, but my dad probably isn't going to like you."

I grin from ear to ear, knowing how much he will dislike me. Hell, he already does, he's just not aware of how badly, but he's about to find out.

Chapter Twenty-Three

Rocco

The way Matt keeps straightening his shirt has my eyes narrowing. "He likes the buttons in line with my zipper," he clarifies, as if sensing my eyes on him.

I choke on thin air. Jesus fucking Christ, he's serious. Just how controlling is this prick?

"You can hang your jacket on there." He points to the hook beside the door, and I shuck off my leather jacket and hang it, then glance down at my signature white T-shirt and jeans. My combat boots are at least laced up and my T-shirt is clean, despite the way my tattoos give the opposite impression.

Maybe I should have researched their family life more than I did. I never delved into the background of their dynamics, and now I'm realizing what a mistake that was because there's so much more at play here, and I don't like the unknown.

The family photos in the foyer have my jaw aching from clenching it so tight. The life in Hallie's eyes isn't there, her gaze despondent, and she's not the girl I know and love. "That's my mom." I turn to face Matt, and a flush creeps over his cheeks. "She's your English teacher, right?"

"You never said," I quip back. The accusation in my tone makes me wince because of how unfair I'm being with all the information I'm holding close to my chest.

"I'm sorry. I just ..." He shifts from foot to foot. "Some people want to be my friend because of my mom, ya know?" The redness in his cheeks deepens, and I take pity on him.

"Your mom's hot, and you wanted to make sure I was in it for the right reasons, I get it."

His eyebrows shoot up. "You do?"

I throw my head back on a chuckle. "I do. She's smoking." My eyebrows dance, and he gives me a shove.

"Ew, shut up, that's my mom."

"Matt!" a deep voice ricochets off the wall, and he turns on a wince and his face falls, making every cell in my body come alive for retribution.

"Coming." My best friend swallows hard before tilting his head toward the door. "Come on. He doesn't like to be kept waiting." I'll fucking bet he doesn't.

I grit my teeth as we head toward what I'm guessing is the dining room, and when Matt stops to knock on the door before entering, I almost stumble into his back.

DECEPTION

"Enter."

Christ. I roll my eyes at the prick's ostentatious rules. Just who the fuck does he think he is?

Matt opens the door, and I swear I can feel the frosty atmosphere in an instant. The room is deathly silent, with no warm welcome or camaraderie like I have with my father and brothers. It's like they're strangers, and when my eyes land on the pompous prick that is Gerrard Davis, it takes everything in me not to launch myself across the table and take him out. His broad shoulders fill his shirt, and his hair is cropped in what I can only describe as a military fashion. The way he sits at the head of the table, like he's something of importance, makes me want to chuckle at his self-arrogance, but I refrain from doing so, letting Matt lead the conversation.

"Who's this?" He flicks his finger in my direction without so much as giving me any attention. Big mistake.

Matt shuffles beside me. "He's my friend, Dad. I asked if I could bring someone to dinner."

"Mm ..." He drags his finger over his top lip. "I don't recall you asking."

"I did. I wouldn't just invite someone over." He shuffles from foot to foot.

Gerrard barely gives me a second glance. "Do I know you from somewhere?" Then he turns his attention back to Matt, inspecting him up and down with a sneer.

"Probably." I lift a shoulder, a smile playing on my lips.

"You can take that seat, Roc, next to my mom." Matt gestures toward the second seat along the table that would position Hallie next to Gerrard. Not. A. Fucking. Chance. Instead, I move around the table and pull out the chair beside Gerrard and slide onto it.

Gerrard releases a low growl, and I ignore it while nonchalantly strumming my fingers against the wood of the table.

An awkward laugh leaves Matt as he takes his seat, and we wait for Hallie to arrive.

"Your mother's late *again*." He grits the latter out, making me want to draw my knife and carve into his perfectly crafted face.

"It's not even seven yet," Matt states, and I want to fist bump him for sticking up for Hal.

"She's pushing it fucking close, and she knows how damn angsty I get with poor timekeeping." His hands ball into fists, and that action has the hairs on my neck standing on end.

Matt glances my way and rolls his eyes, and I smirk back at him.

The door opens, and all the air is sucked from my lungs as she appears. Her beauty is captivating, and her bubbly personality is radiating. My heart hammers at the enormity of the moment as her eyes latch onto mine. Her body jerks, then her eyes flick toward Matt, and her shoulders droop and her lip wobbles. The grip she has on her purse causes her knuckles to whiten, and when her eyes fill with unshed tears, I clutch the table to stop myself from comforting her.

"Where the fuck have you been? You know I don't like to be kept waiting!" She stiffens at Gerrard's accusing tone, and my gaze snaps to his. Every muscle in my body becomes stiff with the pressure of staying in my seat.

She clears her throat. "My apologies." She glances at her watch. "I'm not late; it's not seven yet."

"Mom?" Matt looks up to her, pleading for her compliance, and she bends and plants a loving kiss on his head before ruffling his hair.

"It's okay, buddy. I'm here now. No harm done."

"This is my friend, Roc." He holds his hand out in my direction, and she makes no move to acknowledge me.

"Sit! The fucking meal will be getting cold," Gerrard barks as he points to the place set beside me.

Hallie jumps, and her lips pull into a thin line as she heads my way. When she slides into the seat beside me, I place my hand on her knee beneath the table, and she brushes me off. Her steely glare would have any other man's balls shriveling, but mine only tighten in need. I return my hand and squeeze her thigh in warning.

"Roc is the friend I told you about."

"The one who always worked weekends so he couldn't come over when I invited him for dinner?" she asks as I circle my finger over her thigh.

Matt laughs. "Yeah, him."

The door to the dining room opens, and the servers begin bringing in the food, and I'm fucking grateful for their interruption. I lean forward and tilt my body as an excuse to whisper into Hallie's ear. "Don't be mad, Little Red." My voice comes out pleading, but her jaw sharpens, and she scoffs, then turns her head away from me. The action causes a wave of sickness to settle in my stomach. I knew this would be a shitshow, but still, enduring it is something else. I can practically feel the hate rolling off her, and worse, disappointment too. "Hal?" I try again when she pushes my hand off her thigh, and she subtly shakes her head.

"Roc works on weekends, isn't that right, Roc?"

"Yeah," I say without shifting my attention from Hallie. The lingering feeling of anxiety looms in my stomach, and my fingers itch to force her attention back on me. To command that she look at me with that desperate, reliable, and trustful look in her eyes I've become accustomed to.

"I don't approve of you wearing red, you know that, and yet you still do it simply to piss me off. Isn't that right?" Gerrard glares in Hallie's direction, and my spine stiffens.

"Rocco's worked for as long as I've known him." Matt cuts in and speaks louder, as if trying to divert the conversation, but Gerrard doesn't so much as shift his attention toward him and stays laser focused on Hallie. Jesus, he pays his kid no attention at all.

"It's good you have work ethic so young," Gerrard says and Hallie flinches. "That way, you will be in a good position to support your wife and family." I don't give him my attention, too drawn to the woman beside me as I once again place my hand on her thigh, desperate to seek the reassurance of her touch. "There's no reason why a woman should work. A man should provide for her, and she should be grateful. Of course, there's always some selfish women with notions of equality in their head, and consequently, they abandon their responsibilities for their own selfish needs." He continues with his drivel. "Wanting to make a show of themselves."

His words don't surprise me, and in all honesty, his beliefs aren't all that much different from the Mafia's, so I'm well aware that in this instance, we might be deemed as similar, but where my father and brothers are old school, I have modern beliefs. I'm fine with my girl working, if that's what she wishes. However, enforcing safety in the workplace for her is another story entirely, and something I need to speak to Hallie about sooner rather than later.

"Can we not do this?" Hallie whispers toward Gerrard and just as quickly looks away. I like the fact her eyes don't linger on him for too long, and my chest puffs out with pride at my girl.

"What? Discuss how you abandoned your son because you wanted to waste your time teaching."

"Dad, please?" Matt implores.

"I think Hallie is an incredible teacher. The way she holds the classroom's attention is impressive."

Hallie jolts at my words, and I narrow my eyes. She fidgets with her hands in her lap and ducks her head, her usual confidence gone. The same woman who commanded a classroom of students is nowhere to be seen, and I hate it. When I turn my attention toward Gerrard, I finally understand. His eyes bore into her with venom, and she sits stoically still as if waiting for something.

"She holds attention all right. You and those horny

teenagers probably want to fuck my wife senseless, and she delights in the fucking attention like a goddamn whore." He slams his fist on the table, causing the cutlery to rattle.

"Dad?" Matt's voice lacks conviction as fury floods my veins. How fucking dare he speak about her like that?

"Just telling it how it is, son. Your mother's an attention-seeking slut." He takes a casual drink of his scotch while glaring toward Hallie.

My body vibrates with a rage I've never felt before as my mind battles to stay in control, and when her soft hand wraps around my tight fists beneath the table, a calmness washes over me and I open my eyes, not realizing I'd closed them. She looks directly at me, and I see it all. She's pleading with me not to make a scene, and I fucking hate it.

As much as it pains me to hear the vitriol roll off the fucker's tongue, I've no choice but to endure it. Like she does.

For now, at least.

I exhale deeply and turn my attention toward Gerrard. "You're divorced, right?"

His eyes snap to mine, for the first time tonight giving me his full attention, but he doesn't speak, as if not seeing me as worthy of a response.

"Right?" I try again. "Because you called Hallie your wife, and she isn't." I sit back in my chair with a cocky confidence when the vein on his temple pulsates.

He breathes through his nostrils as Hallie draws circles on the back of my hand. Her touch alone gives me all the strength I need to maintain a sense of control that would otherwise be absent.

"Look, kid, I don't know who the fuck you are, but don't come in my house all cocky, spewing shit you know nothing about." His glare is deadly, but I've seen worse. Much worse.

"Gerrard," Hallie tries to intervene, but I squeeze her hand to stop her, even though my heart is doing somersaults for the only woman to ever put herself on the line for me.

I lean forward. "You don't know me yet, but you will." I smirk back at him.

His eyes narrow as he leans forward. "Is that a fucking threat?"

My smile grows wider. "A promise, Gerry." I wink.

He flinches at my nickname for him. One I know he hates.

It's the same one my brothers use to ridicule him.

His face reddens and his nostrils flare. "Matt, get this piece of shit out of my house," he spits out, and I chuckle at his outburst. "You, stay the fuck there." He points toward Hallie, and my body locks up tight. There's no way I'm leaving her here.

"I have nothing to discuss with you, Gerrard," she snaps.

He leans over the table, his stare menacing. "Well, I've a lot to discuss with you. Starting with the welfare of our son, or are you choosing to abandon your responsibilities again?" The spite in his tone is evident, and she flinches, making me want to take my knife to him as punishment.

She blows out a deep breath, then bends down, fumbling with her purse on the floor. "Please go." I shake my head, my molars grinding. Then she casts her eyes up toward me, and the truth in them strikes me hard. "For all our sakes." She glances toward Matt, who is now waiting for me at the door. The poor kid looks like he can't get the hell out of the house quick enough.

My reluctance drops, and I gift her with a nod. As she turns away from me quickly, I don't miss the flash of relief on her pretty face. Gerrard is too busy staring at my girl's tits to notice our exchange, and I fucking hate it.

I hate this.

But I stand and head toward the door.

For Matt.

For Hallie.

Chapter Twenty-Four

Hallie

Seeing Rocco at the dining table with Matt was like a knife slicing through my heart, leaving it in shredded tatters and of no use to anyone. Slowly, it dawned on me that he knew who I was, and that hurt even more.

It felt like our time together had been a lie. All of it was a lie.

From the moment I met him, he's been deceitful, and it's something I'm unwilling to stand for any longer. After spending years being controlled by my husband, and ultimately betrayed, I refuse to let another man treat me that way, no matter how much his touch brings me to life.

I glance toward my son, once again the innocent party in a betrayal that will rock our family to the core, and anger floods my veins.

How could he do this to Matty? To me?

Every time he tried touching me during dinner, I pushed his hand away. Until he questioned Gerrard in my defense, and I felt like I had no choice but to relent and calm the situation down. Knowing how volatile Gerrard can be, I didn't want Rocco or Matty caught in the crossfire.

When Gerrard insisted on me staying behind, I knew I had no choice. My shoulders relaxed the moment Rocco gave in to my plea for him to leave. Gerrard continuously pushes the charade of our son's welfare as an excuse to communicate with me, but he and I both know he's not interested in Matty; he never was. Our son is simply a pawn, and my heart breaks for him.

"Who the hell are you encouraging our son to hang around with?" he spits out the moment the door closes.

Before I can gather my words to tell him that Matty spends ninety-five percent of the time with him as per our court order, he changes his question.

"Why the fuck do you continue this?" He waves his hand in front of me, and I narrow my eyes. "I have money. Come back, and I'll issue you a new black card." His dark stare drills into me, and in the past, I would back down with the intensity of it, but now, I grit my teeth, pissed we're going over old ground yet again. As always, the conversation is not revolving around our son as he suggested.

"I don't want a black card, Gerrard," I snap, then grab my purse from the floor and push my chair back, preparing to leave. My ass is halfway out the chair when he moves so fast I don't see him coming. He jerks me by the arm and hoists me to my feet, then in a move I've become accustomed to, he leans down and presses his face into my neck, breathing me in, and my stomach rolls as the air from his nostrils creeps over me.

It's not lost on me that his touch feels wrong, that the only touch I want is Rocco's.

"We were good together, Hallie; you just need to give us another chance."

Anger surges inside me as I push him back, but he remains unmoving. "I don't need to do a damn thing, Gerrard. We're divorced. You fucked another woman. It's over." He stiffens at the mention of him fucking another woman. He hates it when I bring it up and insists it never happened despite the photographic evidence hand delivered to me, on the morning of our anniversary, no less.

There was no denying his cock slipping inside another woman in the image, nor his cock down her throat, and no matter how much he protests his innocence, photos speak volumes, as does the woman paid off to keep her mouth shut to everyone else after I tracked her down. She identified his scar only someone who has been intimate with him would know of.

Gerrard's father is the police commissioner and didn't want his son's indiscretions being made public, so I was summoned to a lawyer's office where I was assured she wouldn't be an issue any longer, as if that would make a difference in my decision to divorce his son.

He grips my breast to the point of pain. "You look like a whore in red." I bite back the wince of hurt his fingers deliver and push against him harder, ignoring the way he grinds his solid cock into my stomach as I do. Sickness wells up inside me, and I whimper at his touch. This only seems to make him more determined as his grip strengthens, causing tears to spring to my eyes.

I raise my leg to deliver a swift knee into his balls, but his work phone buzzes on the table, and I use the distraction to shove him away, hating how I need a hot shower to scrub away his touch.

Without giving him a second glance, I rush toward the door.

In one night, my trust in Rocco has shattered along with my heart. With so much at stake, the decision I need to make soon feels heightened, like a heavy ball weighing me down, and I'm not sure how I can survive it.

Me and our baby.

Chapter Twenty-Five

Rocco

I watch from the shadows as she pulls her car into the drive.

The moment Matt and I left the house, I sent Rafael, my oldest brother, a message asking him to create a diversion that would require Gerrard's immediate attention. I needed to get Hallie out of the house. Leaving her there with him was like a new form of torture I never want to endure again. The piece of shit is an abusive bastard through and through, and keeping my hands off him was like a thinning thread of electrical cable ready to combust into flames at any minute.

Steering my motorbike onto the drive, I park alongside her car, but she doesn't so much as lift her head off the steering wheel at the sound of my engine. My throat constricts at the way her bunched shoulders shake as sobs rack through her. I throw open the car door, and she turns her hazel eyes toward me. They're rimmed in red and full of sorrow, and I hate myself for the part I played in putting it there.

I lean into the car, unclip her seatbelt, and lift her into my arms. "Roc ..." Her mouth falls open as I deposit her on my bike. "What are you ..." I maneuver her leg so she's straddling it while I walk around the back and make sure her ass isn't on display. "Rocco?"

Then I throw my leg over my bike, tug her hips toward me, and grab her hands and place them beneath my leather jacket. I hold them against my chest while she continues to protest. "Hold on tight, Little Red."

I rev the engine, delighting in the squeal that leaves her and the way she stiffens against my back while clinging to me as I reverse out of the driveway.

Then I open the throttle and speed off down the street. With my girl pressed against me, I weave in and out of the traffic and head out of town. If my girl thinks this is over, she's about to learn we're only just starting.

Hallie

My hair blows in the breeze, and my body feels alive as I huddle against him, breathing in the smell of his leather jacket and his sandalwood cologne as we make our way out of town.

I've never been on a motorbike before, nor do I think I should be on one right now, but I need to come up with a plan, and soon. Yet as we head farther into the darkness, my mind becomes less and less foggy. All that matters right now is the man who holds my life in his hands.

The steady beat of his heart thumps beneath one of my palms while the other clings to his belt.

"Hold on tighter, Hal." Rocco darts around a truck and causes nervousness and exhilaration to flow through me. He takes me to new heights and holds me there with him. He allows me to soar while always protecting me. And this feeling I get when I'm with him, I never want it to end. But how can it possibly continue?

How can I be in love with someone so young?

How can I have fallen for someone who lied to me so easily?

My student.

My son's best friend.

"You're fucking mine, Little Red. You hear me?" he shouts above the roar of the engine, as if hearing my thoughts.

"I refuse to let you go!"

And the truth is, I don't want him to.

Chapter Twenty-Six

Hallie

Rocco pulls into a dirt covered pull-off, and with only the trees and silence surrounding us, I realize I've no clue where we are.

When he stands, I feel the loss of his warmth and detest the way I long for its return. I turn on the seat and move to stand, but he steps forward, blocking me.

"Hal? Look at me."

Fighting back tears, I turn toward the trees, attempting and failing miserably to compose myself as another tear streams down my cheek. The feeling of losing control of my life is soul destroying. "Little Red, please don't cry," he whispers, and a sob catches in my throat at the gentle tone he uses to speak to me. Such a contrast from Gerrard's threatening one.

His fingers lift and turn my chin, forcing me to face him, and when our gazes meet, guilt pours from him, and that only makes it more difficult to keep my emotions in check.

"Shhh. It's going to be okay." He swipes away the tears one after the other. "I only ever want you to cry for me, you hear me? That way, I can always fix it." My heart skips a beat while I give in to each of his words.

I don't know how much time passes while he holds my face in the palms of his hands, but his presence and willingness to comfort me ground me, instilling in me the difference between Rocco and Gerrard. One was happy to break me and never willing to piece me back together while the other reluctantly breaks me but insists on making me whole again.

"I'm going to make everything right, Hallie. I promise."

I try to shake my head, but he holds me in place, and when I move to push him back, he doesn't budge. "You need to learn you're mine, Little Red."

With all the truths I've come to know today and him telling me I need to learn, a red haze flashes before me, and this time when I push him, I put all my anger and hurt behind it, causing him to stumble back.

I'm conflicted; I want him, but in this moment, I hate him.

The fury in the air is evident between us as he glares back at me with equal venom, and I force myself to remain unmoving.

Why does he have to be the balm that soothes me?

With his eyes locked on mine, he fumbles with his belt and jeans, and my mind is slow to pick up on what is happening. He steps forward, and I let him. "I know you're pissed, Little Red, but you need to let it out. This is happening."

I grind my teeth together.

"Give it to me," he coaxes, and I push him again with a scream that echoes through the trees.

My fists hammer against his chest, but he withstands it all. Then his fingers dig into my chin, pinching it and forcing me to open my mouth as his lips slam against mine in a savage kiss. I bite at his lip, but he doesn't budge, forcing me to accept his tongue as a deluge of copper flows between us.

His kiss is feverous, full of control and power. Full of a passion igniting in the throes of his betrayal as I kiss him back harder, biting his lip harder to punish him for the hurt he caused. He pulls back and swipes away the blood, and my heart stills, knowing I caused it.

He chuckles maniacally. "That's it, Little Red, give me your pain." Then he slams his lips against mine harder than before, attacking me wildly while his hand trails up my thigh and under my dress, heading toward my damp panties. We ravish one another with brutality. I bite him, and he growls, then I claw at his bare skin, and he takes it willingly. I bite him harder, longing to mark him further.

Two savage lovers spiraling out of control.

The power of his deception becomes our undoing.

Rocco

Our passion for one another brings with it a force so powerful and a love so strong it would defeat any obstacle put in our way.

I glide my hands up her dress and graze my fingers over the fabric of her wet panties, and my cock jumps at the impact of her heat. "Your pussy is dripping for me, Little Red." She whines into our kiss. Then I tear the lace from her and swallow down the gasp escaping her pouty lips.

She helps me tug my cock from my boxers, and the way we both fumble with desperation for one another makes my cock drip with need. "Fuck, you need my cock to fill you. Don't you?"

"Yes." Her head falls back as I place kisses down the column of her neck, pulling at her innocent skin to mark her as I do.

I line my cock up to her hole, but pause and wait for her to say the words she knows I want to hear.

She lifts her head to face me, and her sharp gaze pierces through me with a glimmer of hatred I'm prepared to accept. "Yes, Daddy. I want your cock to fill me."

"Good girl." I smooth the hair from her pretty face and rear back and position one hand on her ass to hold her in place, then slam inside her hard. Her head falls back in an instant, and I revel in the swell of her tits in the dress, bouncing with each brutal thrust.

Her pussy molds around me perfectly as I deliver slam after slam into her perfect, wet heat.

"Are you Daddy's good girl, Little Red?"

She moans at my words as my hips keep pumping.

"Are you?"

"Yes. Yes, I'm your good girl."

"You better be. I'm gonna punish you so bad for trying to push me away, Little Red."

"Oh god."

I throw my head back as sweat drips down my spine. Her pussy becomes tighter by the second, on the verge of convulsing. "That's right. Come on my thick cock, be Daddy's perfect little slut for me."

Her lips part on a strangled cry, and my filthy words help to push her over the edge, and her pussy muscles tighten around me. "Fuck, Little Red wants me to put a baby in her belly, don't you?"

As I slam inside her harder, I struggle to rein in the need to come. "Don't you?" I roar as my balls pull up.

"Yesss! I want your baby," she screams with conviction while my cock pulsates deep inside her, and I close

DECEPTION

my eyes and will it to take form. I will it with the same confidence she screamed, and meet it like for like.

"I need you pregnant, Hal," I whisper into the crook of her neck, and she shivers. The desperation in my voice is evident as the enormity of my situation takes its toll. "Please give me a fucking baby," I beg against her ear. "Please."

Chapter Twenty-Seven

Hallie

Rocco pulls out of me, leaving a sticky trail of cum dripping from me, and before I can slip off the bike, he spins me around. "Hold on to the handles, I'm going to fuck you from behind."

I glance over my shoulder while my hands scramble to find the handles. My lips part in awe of him as he steps up to straddle the bike while he fists his cock. Our combined cum drips from his cock, and I squirm with my ass up in the air. The man is bad boy personified, with tattoos creeping out of the top of his white T-shirt, leather jacket, and his ripped jeans around his thighs as he positions his thick, veiny cock to my pussy. Throw in the blood smeared on his cheek from his punctured lip, and I submit with ease.

"Push back on me, Hallie. Show Daddy how much you want this thick cock to fill you." He fists himself, bucking into his hand wildly, and desire flows from me. "Hallie!" he bites out as the muscles on his neck coil tight.

"I want to fuck my cum back into you, Hal."

Oh Jesus, that's hot. "Please, please. Daddy."

He bites into his bottom lip, and his nostrils flare as he points his cock toward me. "That's it, fucking beg, Little Red."

"I want it." I push back so the tip of his cock grazes my crack. Then he delivers a sharp slap to my bare ass cheek. "Fucking greedy slut."

I push back again. "Yes. Greedy for you, Daddy. I want it to stretch me."

A guttural groan leaves his lips, and his free hand lands on my spine. With my ass up in the air, he agonizingly slowly pushes inside me, my pussy still swollen.

"Good. So fucking good." He hisses as he slides inside. "So. Fucking. Good."

He wraps one hand around my hair like a rein, and when he bottoms out, his boots crunch against the gravel as he widens his stance. Then he rears back and surges forward again and again.

"I'm doing it, Hal. I'm fucking my cum deep inside you." The growl in his tone makes me arch my back in pleasure.

Spittle lands on my ass, and my lips part when his thumb grazes over my forbidden hole, and I tense up.

"You're mine!" He pushes it inside with no further warning, and before I can protest to the burn taking place inside me, he moves his thumb in motion with his cock, and instead of feeling any discomfort, a wave of pleasure swirls inside me at the fullness.

"You like that?"

He slams inside me again.

"You like feeling my thumb in your tight little ass?"

His thrusts become violent.

"You're mine to play with, Little Red."

Stars float in front of my eyes as pleasure consumes me.

"Yours," I whisper as his warmth spreads through me.

"My little red."

Chapter Twenty-Eight

Rocco

I drive slowly toward the cabin, and my grip tightens on her, worried she won't hold on to me properly as I drive the winding roads toward my lair.

After Hallie came again while I fucked her ass with my thumb, she was like Jell-O, and the last thing I wanted was for my girl to get hurt.

If she thinks she can leave me, then she's about to learn otherwise. I'll just keep her here until I fuck my baby into her and she has no choice but to accept me into her life.

Besides, the clock is ticking, and before long, my father will want me to step up and play happy fucking families with a girl I have no intention of touching, let alone marrying. The thought repulses me and sends a tsunami of hatred through my body. I belong to Hallie, and she belongs to me. Nobody touches us but each other.

I turn onto the side road and smile at the camera, knowing it will open the concealed entrance to my property, obscured by the naked eye with strategically planted trees.

"Nearly there, Little Red," I whisper as I lift her hand to my lips and kiss her fingers while weaving through the forest.

When my cabin comes into view, Hallie straightens. "Where are we?"

I park my bike, cut the engine, and push out the kickstand. "My cabin."

"I can't stay here." Her head darts around, and she looks adorable as panic sets in.

I chuckle at her cute defiance. Especially when she crosses her arms over her chest and pouts.

"Of course you can."

I lift her from the bike like a child and place her on her feet. She grabs my arm to stabilize herself, then just as quickly detaches from me with a huff. I allow her the petulant act for now, knowing we have a lot to iron out between us.

"I-I can't stay here tonight, Rocco!" She stomps her foot, but I ignore her outburst and head toward the door. I glide my hand over the security screen at the side of the door, and the moment it unlocks, I step inside.

Immediately, the tension falls from me, and I relax in my space. The fact she's here with me is the perfect scenario I've been waiting for.

Hallie

I follow him inside, ready to protest, but my breath is taken away by the view before me. "Holy shit." I gasp.

He spins to face me, and an all-consuming smile encompasses his face, so bright and carefree if I wasn't already breathless, I would be now.

Then he slips his leather jacket off his shoulders and places it onto the back of a couch while I stare toward the glass doors framing the back of the cabin. My feet head toward them, taking in the view of the treetops. It's like we're suspended in midair.

A balcony wraps around the cabin, and a couch and blankets beneath a covered deck have me longing to position myself there.

"Champagne okay?"

I freeze on his words and spin to face him. He's in the open-plan kitchen, with not a care in the world, asking me if I want champagne like we're celebrating something. I shake off the thought and question him.

"Champagne, seriously?"

He shrugs a shoulder with a smirk, then pops open the bottle, sending a deluge of bubbles over the brim. "I could pour it on you and lick it off?"

I shake my head. "I don't want champagne, Rocco. I want to go home, right fucking now!" I scream as I point toward the door.

"Tough." He shrugs, angering me further.

"Tough?"

"Tough. You're staying here." Staring back at me, he dares me to argue.

Anger floods me. "I want to go home."

"No!" He clamps his mouth shut and glares at me, and I swear I hear his teeth grind.

I seethe through my nose. "This is kidnapping. You know that, right?"

"Okay." He shrugs again.

"Okay?" My mouth falls open. "I'm being serious, Rocco." Tears spring to my eyes. I'm tired and hurt and just let him fuck me on his motorbike. I want to shower and curl up in my bed while I try to understand how my life has become a torrent of never-ending turmoil, and come up with a plan on how to deal with it.

His eyes hold mine hostage, and the air between us thickens. "So am I," he growls, and the hairs on the back of my neck stand on end.

"You lied to me," I whisper.

His hardened features soften. "You wouldn't have wanted me otherwise."

I shudder at his words.

DECEPTION

"I might be young, Hallie. But I'm not naïve. If you found out I was your son's best friend, you would have tried to end us. I was trying to make things easier."

"Easier?" I scoff.

"Exactly. Matt loves me already." He grins as if proud.

"As a best friend!" I spit in outrage.

"He'll get used to us."

I shuffle from foot to foot, knowing I hold a secret too. Knowing even if I try to end us, Rocco will always be connected to me.

"I know it's not ideal. But you're my ideal, Hallie, and I want to be yours too. Me, you, and our baby." His breath flutters over me, and I realize he's in front of me. "I love you. I know you're going to think that's crazy and too soon. But from the moment I laid eyes on you, you're the only woman I have ever seen. All I want is a chance to prove to you I can be everything you need."

"I don't know what I need," I murmur as my lip quivers.

He takes my face in the palms of his hands. "Yes you do, Hallie. You need me to be strong for you, protective and loving. You need me to take you to new heights so we can soar together. You need me to carve out our future and guide you toward it. I can deliver everything you need, but it would be so much easier if you allowed me to do it."

"What if I don't?" I hold his eyes, and he licks his top lip slowly, as if calculating his next move. His pupils darken and his body tenses, but the change in him doesn't scare me, it's something he does when he becomes dominant, when the gentle Rocco disappears.

"I'll take what we both want eventually anyway." Meaning, he's giving me no choice.

He tilts my head to place a kiss on my forehead, then steps back, taking my heart with him. Then he swoops down and takes me in his arms, causing me to squeal as he marches me through the cabin and kicks open a door. My eyes dart around the room, taking in the huge wooden bed, and before I have a chance to look further, we're in a bathroom.

Placing me on the floor, he turns the taps to the shower on. The way his muscles flex and his abs contract as he drops his clothes to the floor has my pussy clenching despite already having had sex twice in the past hour.

His cock springs free from his boxers, standing tall and proud with a bead of pre-cum on the tip that has me wanting to drop to my knees and pleasure him.

His chuckle breaks my train of thoughts. "Arms up, Little Red."

I respond willingly, and he slips my dress up and over my head, dropping it to the floor, then he slaps my ass.

"Shower."

Knowing he's watching me, I spin on the balls of my feet and put an extra swing into my step as I walk toward the shower.

The water hits me, and I cry out in delight, basking in the warmth splashing against my skin, unraveling the tension built inside me. The day's worries and emotions are washed away as Rocco lathers me with his shower gel.

DECEPTION

My breasts are tender when his palms swipe over them, and I can't help but push back against him as his hands work up toward my throat. "You're a good girl letting me take care of you." He hums in my ear, and the suds slide down my body and into the drain.

One hand roams over the softness of my stomach, causing me to flinch and push his hand away at the discomfort in my bones. Rocco places his hand back on my stomach and tightens his palm there. "I told you I'm obsessed with your body, Hallie, and I mean it. Don't push me away from what's mine," he grits out, not realizing the enormity behind his actions.

Then he spins me to face him. His palms flatten on the tiles next to my head, caging me in. "Have you any idea how much I want to punish you for pushing me away?" His gray eyes darken while they bore into mine, making me squirm on the spot, and when his cock twitches, my eyes dart there.

"I can guess."

His lips tip up into a smirk, then his gaze trails over me, heating me with the intensity of his stare.

When his body freezes and the cords of his neck tighten, I lift my head toward his face to try to decipher the change in him.

He stares at my chest, and I glance down, only now realizing the bruising over my breast from Gerrard's heavy hand. I jolt and try to step back, but my back is already flush against the wall.

"Who?"

I close my eyes to shut out the darkness in his voice, knowing what I'm about to say might change everything.

"I asked you a question, Hallie. I expect a fucking answer!" he booms, making me flinch at the venom in his tone.

A chill takes over my body, and goose bumps spread over me.

I drop my head and wrap my arms around my center, bending as if to protect myself, which I know is silly. If there's one thing I know and believe, Rocco's protective of me and would never hurt me. Not physically, anyway.

Instantly, he softens, so quick to change to accommodate how I feel.

He lets out a deep exhale, then turns and walks out of the shower. Returning with a fluffy white towel in one hand, he switches off the shower jets with the other.

When he holds out his palm, my hand finds his. He gently pulls me toward him and wraps me in the towel, then lifts me into his arms, and I bury my head into his neck and breathe in his scent to seek comfort.

He walks us through the bathroom and into his bedroom, then stops at his bed and sits down, cradling me against him.

"Tell me, how did you get the bruise, Little Red?" There's not a hint of anger in his tone, and my mind becomes jumbled at how calm he appears because, deep inside, I know he's anything but.

I know the extreme Rocco. I see the danger lurking in his eyes. I've experienced the threat of violence he's capable of, but right now, he's as far away from the Rocco I know him to be.

Some might say this is the sign of a sociopath.

But I'm grateful for it, because he's the Rocco I need him to be.

And I love him for it.

Rocco

I'm not even sure how I'm containing the anger as it surges through my veins like a tsunami of poison, but I am. For her.

There's not a shadow of doubt in my mind that if I reacted how I wanted to that I'd push her away when I so desperately want to keep her. I know what my girl needs, and what she needs is for me to rein in my fury and comfort her.

"Tell me, how did you get the bruise, Little Red?" I gently coax.

Her sparkling hazel eyes meet mine, the green in them flashing as she flicks them over my face, searching for a reason to hold back the information.

I remain impassive.

I've spent years training to be the man I am today. One capable of violence, manipulation, and torture, and when I get my hands on whoever touched her, then my mask of indifference will slip, and I will unleash my fury tenfold. For now, I will protect my girl.

She swallows, and I follow the motion. My cock takes this opportunity to throb with excitement at the prospect of stuffing her small mouth and pushing myself deep inside her throat. As if hearing my thoughts, she wiggles beneath me.

I grasp her chin between my fingers. "Don't try distracting me, Little Red." Her pupils widen at my heavy hand but not in protest—no, my little red likes me treating her roughly.

"Tell me," I bite out, annoyance overtaking me, causing me to feel like a bomb ready to explode.

"Gerrard cornered me when you left," she whispers, and I suck in a sharp breath of air and close my eyes to try to control the red haze overtaking me.

My body tightens to the point of pain, and I snap my eyes open when Hallie slips from my arms and onto the mattress.

"You can't do anything," she states.

I flex my fists and scoff, then slice my eyes toward Hallie.

"You can't," she whispers, with tears in her eyes.

"He bruised you," I spit out, getting to my feet. "He bruised you, and you expect me to do nothing?" The venom in my tone is at full force.

She blows out a deep breath. "He's Matty's father, Rocco. He's also the police commissioner's son. He's a police officer."

I rear back and scoff. "I know who the fuck he is."

It's her turn to scoff this time. "Of course you do," she snipes out. "But you don't realize how much power he has."

"He has power?" I hold her gaze, then lower myself so I'm leaning over her. "Sweetheart, Gerrard Davis is a fucking bug I intend on swatting." My deadly tone creeps in.

"He's Matty's father," she repeats, making me chuckle at her lame attempt to save the prick from my revenge.

She shakes her head. "Rocco, please. You don't understand what he can be like."

I straighten. "Oh, I understand, all right, and he's about to learn the full wrath of my family."

"Wha-what do you mean?"

Past giving a damn about disguising my identity, I decide to unleash the truth on her. "I mean, my family is who keeps Gerrard Davis and all his little fucking minions employed. We're the underground of society. The villains, so to speak."

Her mouth falls open, and I ignore it.

"But let me tell you this. We never hurt innocent women, and we don't touch kids."

She shakes her head. "I don't understand."

"My father is a Mafia don, Hallie. Harrison Davis has been trying to put him away for years."

"The Mafia?" Her lip trembles. "Our families are enemies?"

"No! Not our families. You're mine. The sooner we

get married, the fucking better." A need like never before overcomes me. "You're my family."

It's always been part of my plan to marry her, but now I feel it with a newfound urgency.

She knows who I am. By now, Gerrard would have figured it out too, and that means Matt is about to discover how much his father truly hates me.

It's time to move my plan forward.

Chapter Twenty-Nine

Hallie

Fear swims in my stomach as Rocco furiously types on his phone. His eyes are narrowed, and his taut muscles are bunched tight.

Deep down, I knew there was more to Rocco than meets the eye.

He was never just an average student. The maturity and darkness lurking behind his gaze radiated from him, and the savagery of his behavior was unheard of. But never in my thirty-three years did I expect him to say he was a part of a Mafia family, an integral part of it. If his father is a Mafia don, then I can only assume he plays a key role in the family too.

Just what does that consist of? And where does that leave me and our baby?

A heavy pool of dread ripples through me. The mess

I find myself in is getting darker and deeper by the second.

I watch him type away, taking in the way he sits in the armchair with such dominance it makes me squirm. There's not a doubt in my mind that Rocco wants me and our baby. He wasn't wrong when he said he was obsessed with me; there's simply not another word to describe it.

But now our baby is at the center of what is about to become a war. Our baby's father a student of mine, my son's best friend, and an age gap that will be frowned upon. A family divided, the good and the bad.

My heart constricts at the thought of Matty's reaction. I've already given up so much for my freedom. If he hadn't pushed to stay with his father, I would have relented, and part of me knew he knew it too.

Will he still want to see me when he finds out the truth? That he's about to become a brother in these twisted circumstances.

A sob erupts from me, and Rocco is at my side in a flash.

"Shh, don't cry, Little Red. Everything's going to be okay." He buries his fingers in the back of my hair while he places kisses all over my face. "Daddy's going to take care of you, always."

Then he unwraps the towel, and I open my legs for him to position himself between them.

He nibbles down my neck, a small bite of pain with each tug of my skin, followed by a lick of his soft tongue until he reaches my breasts. He sits back on his heels to watch himself knead them, as if he knows they're tender, yet he can't.

Then he leans forward and laps at my nipple. Taking it into his mouth, he sucks softly while his free hand trails over the bruise on my flesh. He strokes the tarnished skin in a soothing motion, and I thread my fingers through his wayward hair, loving the soft, silky feel to his dark locks while he tastes me.

Will our baby have his dark silky hair or my red curls?

My thoughts are banished when the stickiness of his cock coats my leg, and he slowly rocks back and forth while flicking his tongue over the peaked tip of my nipple.

He groans in pleasure, and I arch my back into him.

"Fuck, you have the best tits ever, Hal."

Moving to the other one, he moans as his lips seek the aching bud.

The pleasure of him sucking on my tit is consuming, and wetness drips from me, and I crave for him to deliver me his dirty words and his thick cock.

"Sooo good." I moan wantonly.

"Fuck yes." He lifts his head and pushes my tits together, playing with my nipples. His calloused hands add a bite of pain to the pleasure as he stares at them in awe, making me feel whole and womanly.

Each insecurity I have, Rocco has banished in a heartbeat.

"Did you feed Matt from these?" he asks, quirking a brow, and I still at his bizarre question.

"N-no, Gerrard didn't want that." I grimace, knowing how ridiculous that sounds. In truth, I was a vulnerable teenage girl who got pregnant by her first boyfriend, and I was grateful Gerrard decided to stand by me, unlike other less fortunate girls my age. My own parents abandoned me, but Gerrard's family offered me an out.

Marry their son and they would take care of us both, seeing us through school and college and helping provide care for Matty. While I never felt good enough for their son, I was always grateful for the way they stepped in and offered me the support my family wouldn't. So, of course, I spent every day reminding myself of the fact I was lucky to have them. So grateful, I would always do as I was told without question, and I indirectly became the perfect obedient little housewife, molded to their satisfaction.

Maybe that's why Rocco and I have such chemistry. Our lives have been dictated too much for us to simply be ourselves.

Gerrard once told me his parents only allowed me to have a college education to brag about how well educated their son's wife was. It was never for me to use in any capacity. It hurt, but it was true. I was never meant to become a teacher; I was never meant to become anything other than what they wanted me to be.

Nothing.

"Fuckkk." Rocco's voice brings me back to the present. "You've no idea how much the idea of feeding from you turns me on." I lift my head off the pillow to find his focus glued to his hands playing with my tits, and suddenly, I want to give him that. I want him to experience everything with me, everything I never got to experience. We will do it all.

"I want that too, Daddy."

Rocco

"I want that too, Daddy." She widens her legs as her eyes fill with insatiable need.

"Do you want to feed Daddy from your big milky tits?"

"Yes," she breathes out, the red creeping over her chest as I push her inhibitions.

"Is your little cunt all nice and wet for Daddy?"

"Yes."

"Show me."

My cock aches, but I refuse to give it attention, so I rest back on my heels as she draws her legs up toward her chest, pushing those glorious full tits higher. "Fuck, you've no idea how hot you look, Little Red." I buck as she spreads her pussy lips to expose her slick hole.

Her innocent pink fingernails stroke over her clit, forcing pre-cum to drip from my slit. I caress her soft legs while she circles her swollen bud, and small sounds of heaven escape her parted lips, each adding fuel to the fire burning deep inside me.

"Do you like watching me play, Daddy?" She licks her lips, and I almost combust, and my fingers tighten on her legs. Holy shit, her dirty talk is hot.

"You know I do," I choke out.

Her index finger moves lower, then she slides the tip in and out of her slick little cunt.

"Fuck, Little Red. That's it, get it nice and wet."

She gasps, and the reddening on her chest increases with her rapid breaths.

"Put your pussy juice on your nipples and let Daddy lick it off."

Her head falls back against the pillow. "Oh god." She complies quickly, using multiple fingers to swipe at her wetness and coat her nipples.

"Always such a good girl, Little Red."

"Yes."

I waste no time in taking hold of her hand and sucking her fingers into my mouth. Her eyes widen, then I slam her wrists above her head, holding her in place with one hand as I position my cock at her slick entrance.

Then, in one sharp snap of my hips, I bury myself deep inside her. My lips wrap around her nipple, and I lap at it, savoring her taste and the softness of her flesh.

Her back arches and her hips rise with each powerful thrust, and the mattress squeaks beneath us. The slapping of our skin and our moans fill the room.

"Your cunt is so tight for me, Little Red."

"Yes."

DECEPTION

"Does my big cock stretching you hurt?"

"Yes. So good." She groans.

"Is Daddy filling you with our baby?"

"Oh god, Rocco."

I slam inside her harder as punishment, earning a cry from her.

"Daddy. Daddy." She rectifies her mistake.

"That's right. Daddy is fucking your little cunt."

"Yes."

"Daddy is sucking on your juicy tits."

"Yes."

"Daddy is filling you with our baby."

Her pussy muscles tighten, forcing my movements to stutter.

"Please."

"Beg. Fucking beg for me to put a baby in you." I grab her chin with my hand and force her to look at me. "Beg me to come inside you and fill you with a baby."

"Please, Daddy."

"Good girl," I praise as my balls ache for release. "Good fucking girl. Make Daddy come, Little Red. Make me come inside your tight little cunt."

"Yesss." Her lips part as she throws her head back, and I suck her tit harder, licking her clean, then her orgasm smashes into her.

A satisfying groan of euphoria is pulled from me as my cum shoots deep inside her, ensuring our future.

Chapter Thirty

Rocco

When I checked my phone earlier to find Rafael and his right-hand man had been trying to contact me to tell me Oblivion—one of our clubs—was on fire, there wasn't a doubt in my mind that Gerrard was behind it, so I pointed Kai in that direction despite knowing the shit it would cause.

After fucking Hallie into a peaceful sleep, I fire my brother a text.

> Me: Any update?

> Rafael: Where are you?

> Me: Any update?

> Rafael: Get your ass home.

Me: I have a wedding to plan.

Rafael: You're joking?

I chuckle, imagining my brother pulling his hair out.

Me: No.

Rafael: Papa is going to kill you.

Me: He'd miss me.

Rafael: He'd live.

Me: Besides, you all need me.

Rafael: We'd manage.

I scoff. As if they could manage without me. When my brother Tommy checked out of our family, I stepped up, even as a teenager, and became everything my brother was incapable of being.

Me: Pretty sure I'm his favorite.

Rafael: Like fuck you are. When's the big day?

I glance over my shoulder toward Hallie's sleeping form. Seeing her mass of red hair splayed out over my pillows and her luscious hips tangled in my sheets has my heart hammering hard.

DECEPTION

Jesus, she's beautiful. And all fucking mine. I refuse to go another day without her by my side.

> Me: Today.

My mind races with everything that needs to fall into place ASAP. I drag a finger over my lip as I contemplate the shit that's about to go down. My brother isn't wrong; my father will go insane, but I'd give my life for Hallie and Matt.

I just hope it doesn't come to that.

> Me: You there?

> Rafael: Your funeral.

> Rafael: Congratulations.

> Rafael: When it's done, get your ass home. You're needed before you die.

I roll my eyes at his dramatics and throw my head back on a dark laugh. When I raise my head, my girl is standing before me with the sheets wrapped around her. The breeze blows them, and fuck if she doesn't look like an angel, my daring red angel.

"What's so funny?" She points toward the phone.

"I told my brother we're getting married."

A choked noise leaves her, and she shakes her head. "Rocco."

I tug her into my lap. "It's happening, Little Red."

"Matty?"

"Will be fine. I'll speak with him."

Her concerned gaze roams over my face. "You're eighteen, Rocco."

"I know. Trust me, I fucking know." I've spent what feels like a lifetime waiting to be eighteen to make her mine.

She chews on her bottom lip. "I don't want to cause a problem between our families."

As she refers to Gerrard as her family, I grind my jaw. Then she shakes her head. "He's Matty's father. You and I both know Gerrard is going to be ...disgruntled." Disgruntled? Crazy, unhinged, frenzied, or apocalyptic are words I would've chosen.

I blink at her innocence and shake my head. "Then let him be disgruntled." I stare into her eyes and try to hide the smirk tugging at my lips. "Let him be fucking disgruntled, and see where it gets him. But I swear to Christ if he lays one more finger on you, I will end him. Matt's biological father or not."

She moves to get off my lap, but I hold her there, determined to see this conversation through, and my fingers dig deeper into her thighs. "You know Matt only lives with him so your divorce went through quicker, right? He wanted you to get away from him."

Her chest rises, she licks her lip, and hurt swims in her eyes as she fiddles with her hands. "I wondered that. He told me and the courts he wanted to live with his dad." She reiterates while trying to hold back the tears forming in her eyes.

"He wanted to protect you. He's more of a man than that piece of shit ever was."

She swallows hard. "Have you any idea how much it hurts to know your son sacrificed himself for your happiness?"

"No, baby, I don't. But I do know Matt is a good, strong guy. You need to give him credit for what he is. He wants you to be happy, if that means with me, then ..." I shrug.

"It's still going to hurt him."

I battle rolling my eyes. In my world, hurting people comes through torture, not small dramas like this.

"And I'll be there for him. I'll be there for you." I place my hand on her stomach. "And one day when you're pregnant, I'll be there for our baby too." I don't miss the way she jerks beneath my touch, something new, something I don't like, and when she pales, I narrow my eyes.

Before I can read too much into it, she sits up straighter and drills me with a sharp look. "No more lies, Rocco." She closes her eyes, and when she reopens them with a renewed vigor, I see her strength and resilience combined. "I refuse to be lied to any longer. I've spent my entire adult life being lied to; I need you to be honest with me."

Nervousness blooms in my chest, and my mouth becomes dry. The last thing I want to do is let her down, but she's not ready for the whole truth, no matter how much she thinks she is, and I refuse to push her away when I have her so close.

"Okay," I whisper, hoping she doesn't see the deceit swimming in my eyes.

"Why is getting married so soon so important to you?"

I lick my lips, and she watches me closely. When her soft hand grazes over my jaw, my body turns to putty under her delicate touch.

"Being part of a Mafia family means there are expectations."

She nods as if understanding, but I doubt she really does. Unless you're in this life, this world of ours, nobody could ever truly understand.

"There's a girl."

The tips of her fingernails dig into my skin, and I welcome the bite of pain. "I'm expected to marry her."

She freezes.

"An arranged marriage?" She tilts her head to study me.

Her nose scrunches and her lip turns up, making me want to laugh at her adorable reaction.

"It's common practice in the Mafia."

"It's archaic."

A chuckle leaves me. "It is, but it's our way of life, and it's expected of me."

"Do you know her?" Her words are laced in a hint of jealousy, and my lips twitch with delight.

"Jealous?"

DECEPTION

Her lips twist, then draw into a straight line, and she raises her chin. "No."

"Right." I laugh, ignoring her blatant lie, then clear my throat. "A deal was struck years ago, and I was the only son left to have her."

"You make her sound like cattle," she snaps.

I look at her pointedly. "She might as well be."

Her lips part. "That's awful."

"No more awful than being forced to marry your first boyfriend in order to keep your kid," I counter, causing her to flinch, then follow my words up with a swift kiss to her forehead. "I'm sorry."

Shaking her head, she swallows hard. "You're right. I'm sorry for judging. D-do you have any feelings toward her?" Worry mars her perfect face, and I hate that it's there.

I stare into her eyes, the green flecks in them so hypnotizing they take my breath away for a second. Can't she see the only love I possess is for her? "No, Little Red." I place a kiss on her lips and bask in the glory of the way her body and her lips follow mine. "I love you. It's only ever been you." Relief washes over her face, and her lips curl into a serene smile I've become indebted to. Then I clear my throat. "I've never met her. But her family is prominent in our world. My marriage to you will cause shock waves."

She makes to move off me, the panic evident in the way her chest rises and her body shudders. "Hallie, chill the fuck out. You need to trust me." Then I palm her face in my hands. "Do you trust me?" I search her face.

"I do," she says with conviction despite her lip quivering.

"Good girl. We're going to get married, and me putting a baby in you will solidify our commitment." I place my hand on her stomach for emphasis and delight in the gasp that escapes her, knowing she has no choice but to comply.

Hallie

"Good girl. We're going to get married and me putting a baby in you will solidify our commitment."

My heart aches at his words.

Until recently, I wasn't sure when I became pregnant, but now I'm certain it was during our first time together.

I was in denial. Being delusional. Especially when I discovered my baby's father was my student, no less.

The repercussions for our indiscretion became tenfold, so I buried my head in the sand.

When Rocco explained about his arranged marriage, jealousy swam in my stomach, an emotion I've only ever felt around him. The way the young girls' eyes would eat him up at school had my teeth aching from grinding them. Every cell in my body wanted to tell them he's mine, but I had to keep it secret.

Until now.

"You're still my student," I blurt out.

Rocco throws his head back on a loud laugh. *Why is he laughing?* "Little Red, if you think that's an issue, then you're sorely mistaken."

"What do you mean?"

"I don't want, nor do I need, to be a student. It was a way of getting close to you." He shrugs. "I'll drop out, no worries."

My mouth falls open at how easily he's banishing his future. "You can't drop out, Rocco."

"Hal, my future is already carved out for me. I don't need school; my father reminds me of it every damn day." He lifts his shoulder, and for the first time since he mentioned being in the Mafia, I look at him, I really look at him.

He's eighteen years old and knows where his future lies—with his family. Whether he likes it or wants a career elsewhere. His life was stolen from him. His path has been carved without having any options.

"Hey ..." He tilts my head to face him. "I like my life. I never wanted to pursue school."

"But what if you did?" I whisper.

"I don't. Besides, my father might be our don and a dick, but he always wants what's best for us."

"And what's that? What's best for you?"

"You, Hallie. You're what's best for me. My father will see that, and he'll want it too."

A tear slips from my eye, and I hate feeling so weak, but I can't help it. "I'm scared."

"I once told you I'll catch you when you fall, Little Red, and I meant it. It takes a fighter to admit they're scared, Little Red. But it takes a warrior to defeat it, and you're a warrior, Hal." He swallows, and his Adam's apple slides back up his throat slowly. "Let's be warriors together." It's the closest Rocco has come to expressing to me he's scared, and something tells me he would never admit feeling it. Maybe it's a weakness in the Mafia, but knowing we're going into battle together has me throwing my leg over his waist with confidence. Then I drop the bedsheet and let it pool to my waist.

His pupils blow wide as I grind against him, then I lift both of my tits in offering. "Feed from me, Daddy," I plead, knowing he needs this comfort as much as I do.

"Fuck," he groans, as I arch my back when his lips close around my nipple, and his hands pump the flesh. "Daddy loves feeding from you, Little Red."

I dig my nails into his scalp as he sucks hungrily and frees his cock, lining himself up to my hole. When I slam down on him, his eyes roll on the impact.

The wind is knocked from me as I close my eyes. Then I ride him hard and push aside the secret I harbor. Something inside me tells me not to give it away too soon.

The fallout is about to be catastrophic.

Chapter Thirty-One

Hallie

"Where are we going?" I glance around the town in bumfuck nowhere. After we showered and dressed this morning, Rocco pulled an SUV out of the garage below the cabin and drove us toward a town I never knew existed. It's quaint and full of country character, out of sorts compared to the city, but I love it already.

"We're going for breakfast; it's going to be a busy day, and I want you to eat before we start."

His eyes never leave the road, avoiding making eye contact.

"What's happening today?"

"We're getting married."

I splutter on a choked laugh. He's kidding.

"Today?!" I glance around as if a wedding entourage will spring up from nowhere.

He pulls into a parking lot of a rundown diner, switches off the engine, and turns to face me. "Today." He smirks.

I glance down at the same red dress I wore to dinner two nights ago. "I can't get married in this."

Rocco grins back at me. "I want you to."

"You do?"

He nods. "It was the first thing I saw you in. It's how you became my little red." My mind races as I try to recollect the memory of what I wore the first night we met. I'm pretty sure it was a black dress, but I don't correct him.

Besides, Gerrard always hated me in red; he said it made me look like a whore. It would be a big fuck you to him.

I clear my throat. "So, when is this wedding taking place?"

"Our wedding is taking place in"—he checks his watch—"a little over an hour." My mouth drops open. "There." He points toward a little white chapel down the road, and I sink back into the seat. I love it.

When I married Gerrard, I was never asked what I wanted for a wedding. I wouldn't have picked the outlandish princess dress they chose to disguise my pregnancy, nor the elaborate golf club to host the ceremony at.

What I would have picked was something very much like the chapel down the street. I remember sending Sharna an image of one I loved as a suggestion for her wedding.

"It's perfect," I murmur.

Rocco's smile encompasses his handsome face, then he throws open the SUV door, and before I can open my own, he's there helping me out.

Rocco

Taking Hallie to my favorite place to eat means everything to me. I can't wait to bring her here with Matt and our baby—our little family eating in a booth like normal families do.

I've been brought up with luxury and fine dining, but I've always shied away from any of that, forging my own path. My father allowed me the freedom to dress how I like and ride a motorbike while my brothers were chauffeur driven for one of two reasons. One, he didn't want to push me away like he had my brother Ricardo, and two, I was the youngest of the family, so the chances of needing me to become the heir were slim. Therefore, I didn't matter too much. Not that he ever made me feel that way, but the freedom I was allowed compared to my brothers proved it.

So, while my brothers were robbed of their freedom, I was given mine with a veiled understanding that I would one day marry the girl expected of me. Of course, there was only ever me who knew that day would never come.

The bell chimes as I open the diner door and step inside, pulling Hallie in with me.

Celia spins on her tennis shoes and faces me before registering my girl. Then she claps. "There she is!"

Celia is in her midsixties, with her silver hair in a bun, a typical diner waitress uniform, and an apron around her waist. She practically springs toward us, making me chuckle at her overenthusiasm. Then she throws her arms around a shell-shocked Hallie, and I grin from ear to ear. "Oh my, she's beautiful. Isn't she beautiful?"

"She is." I nod.

"Rocco, you have yourself a beauty right here. You better look after her, do you hear me?" She glares at me.

"Yes, ma'am."

Then she swats at my arm. "You charmer, you. Come, I have saved you the booth you like." She takes Hallie by the hand, and I follow behind, chuckling at the way Hallie looks like a deer caught in the headlights. Celia practically pushes Hallie into the booth, and I follow, taking up the space beside her. She quickly hands over the menus while her bright-blue eyes trace every part of Hallie, as if in awe at finally getting to meet the girl I've told her so much about.

"I'll be back in a few minutes to take your order." Celia winks, then rushes off toward the kitchen.

"You know there's a space right there, don't you?"

DECEPTION

Hallie points toward the vacant seat in front of us, and I widen my legs farther.

"I like to be next to you." I grin.

"Of course you do." She rolls her eyes. "What's all that about?" She waves her hand toward Celia's retreating form.

"I told her about you."

"I gathered."

"I needed to tell someone about Daddy's little obsession." Her breath hitches when I bury my face in her neck, placing gentle kisses beneath her ear, and she squirms in her seat.

"More like Daddy's deception."

I chuckle at her words. "That too." She has no idea how deep the deceit runs, and hopefully, she will never find out, but with my plans falling into place, we will be too far gone for it to make a difference.

Celia clears her throat. "Do you two love birds know what you'd like to order?"

"We'll have two Cokes with ice and lemon and two bacon cheeseburgers and smothered fries," I say, without lifting my head from Hallie's neck.

"I'll be right back with those drinks." She giggles as she retreats.

I nip at Hallie's neck, leaving a mark, and she pulls back. "Seriously, Rocco? You're marking me?"

"Little Red, you've no idea what mark I plan on leaving on you tonight."

She pulls back with furrowed brows, and I grin.

"Here we are, two Cokes with ice and lemon." Celia places the drinks down on the table, then claps. "So, tell me, when's the little one due?"

Hallie

"So, tell me, when's the little one due?" Celia asks, and I spit my Coke across the table, and Rocco throws his head back on a loud chuckle that gathers attention from the other diners.

"She's not pregnant," Rocco says. "Yet." My stomach twists with the lie I hold while I asked him to always tell me the truth.

"Oh, I assumed the whole shotgun wedding thing was because there was a bun in the oven."

I mean, the woman isn't wrong, not really. I grimace at the thought.

"Nope, just want to lock my girl down." Rocco grips my knee.

"I can see why," Celia says with a warm smile. "Well, I'll get those burgers over here, then leave you kids to it and see you over there in ..." She glances at her watch. "Half an hour."

As soon as she leaves, Rocco explains without me needing to ask him. "She's a witness."

"Oh." I chew into my bottom lip, the reality of what we're about to do taking its toll.

"You good with that?" He searches my face.

"Of course." I smile back as worry claws at me. "I haven't even done anything with my hair." I comb my fingers through my unruly loose waves.

"What the hell's wrong with your hair?" His eyebrows knit together, and I giggle at the seriousness in his tone. Never once has he made me feel anything less. Not once has he met my insecurities with anything but love, and has always showered me with compliments.

"You're fucking perfect, Hallie."

I bite into my lip. "Thank you, Daddy."

Burning desire fills his eyes, like a switch has been flipped. "I'm going to fuck my wife senseless, you know that, right?"

"I'm counting on it." I smile back as I press a kiss to the corner of his mouth, causing him to growl and tighten the hold on my thigh.

Chapter Thirty-Two

Hallie

I never envisaged being walked down the aisle by my future husband, but that's what I'm doing.

The little white chapel is quaint, yet full of life. As soon as we stepped inside, I felt at peace. With a sea of red roses lining the aisle, we walk down to get to the altar.

An officiant stands at the center podium and greets Rocco with a handshake, then Rocco claps the back of a tall man with broad shoulders who has dark eyes trained on me. The intensity of his stare has me swallowing.

"This is Silas, my right-hand man."

I'm not sure what that means, but Rocco must deem him important to have him here, so I hold out my hand to greet him. "Nice to meet you, Silas."

He takes my hand and pulls it toward his mouth. "The pleasure is all mi—"

Rocco snatches my hand away and pushes him,

forcing him to stumble back. "Get your fucking hands off her."

Silas steps back with his hands held up. "Chill, Roc."

The nickname he gives him sends a rush of warmth through me, knowing Matty greets him the same way. Something Rocco has clearly bestowed on him too.

"Shall we start?" The officiant breaks the tension.

"Yes!" Celia smiles widely, and I can't help but mirror it. Her enthusiasm is infectious.

"Did you have to fucking bring her too? You know she doesn't leave me alone, right?" Silas whispers into Rocco's ear.

"I know." He smirks back.

"Bastard."

"We are gathered here today ..."

Rocco

The officiant seems to go on forever, when all I want is to say is "I do," then fuck my wife into oblivion.

After withdrawing the rings from the inside pocket of my leather jacket, I slide hers on her finger, and she does the same for me, our eyes never leaving one another's. My heart aches at her beauty, my wife.

"I now pronounce you husband and wife."

Thank fuck for that.

I slam my lips against hers, pulling her toward me in one swoop, and swallow down her gasp of surprise.

The exhilaration at knowing she's mine has my head spinning with triumph.

Everything is falling perfectly into place.

When I pull back from Hallie, she sways on her feet, and I steady her. We're both breathless, swimming in the intoxication of one another as Silas and Celia sign the relevant paperwork. Silas slaps me on the back, and I step forward to sign, then Hallie does the same without pause, and I revel in her compliance.

"Congratulations, lovebirds. Now I need to get back to my shift." Celia hugs Hallie, and I bend to let her kiss my cheek.

"Go wait outside." I cut Silas a look and point toward the door, and the tip of his lips tells me he understands.

"We done here?" I turn to the officiant.

"Yes, sir." He places the marriage license in an envelope and gives it to Silas.

"Good. You can leave with Silas."

"Rocco!" Hallie snipes, but I ignore her.

"Come on, old man." Silas guides him out the door, and the moment it closes behind them, I turn to face my girl.

"Take the dress off, Little Red. Daddy wants to fuck you."

Chapter Thirty-Three

Hallie

My jaw almost hits the floor as I spin around the chapel in confusion. "Here?"

"Here." He nods.

"You're insane."

"We've established that. Do you need me to cut it from you?" He withdraws his knife, and wetness pools between my legs.

Knowing I have nothing else to wear, I shake my head.

"Good girl, now drop the dress. Don't make Daddy ask you again."

I grab the hem of the dress and lift it over my head. I'm naked underneath, but something tells me Rocco planned that. Then I drop it to the floor, and he whistles lowly. "Mrs. Marino ..." He winks while his chest puffs out.

Color rushes to my cheeks with the way his hooded eyes devour me.

"Fuck, my cock is so hard." He grunts while stroking over his jean-clad bulge.

"Turn around and get on your hands and knees on the steps."

I spin around and lower myself to the floor, not missing the flash of silver that gleams as I do. His words come back to me. *"Little Red, you've no idea what mark I plan on leaving on you."*

"Rocco?"

He leans over me, then I hear his zipper. "Shhh. It's okay."

The tip of his knife trails down my spine, leaving goose bumps in its wake.

"Is it going to hurt?" I whisper.

"Probably."

I ball my hands into fists, waiting for the pain to come when I realize I can't grip onto the floor. He caresses my ass cheeks, and I push back against him, then he delivers a harsh slap, and I jolt at the force.

"I'm going to spank you, and I want you to count them for me. Do you understand, Little Red?"

"Yes, Daddy."

He hisses, and my core clenches at how much he enjoys me calling him daddy.

His palm hits my ass, and my skin burns.

"One, Daddy."

Smack.

"Two, Daddy."

DECEPTION

"You look damn good kneeling at the altar for Daddy."

Smack ...

I clench as my ass throbs with each delicious spank he delivers. One after the other, barely giving me a chance to count the next.

"Eight, Daddy."

Smack.

"So good on your hands and knees at the altar, begging for me to fill your little cunt with my cum."

"Nine, Daddy."

"You need Daddy to impregnant you, don't you?"

Smack.

"Ten, Daddy."

A slice through the skin of my ass causes my body to still at the brutality of it, then it's followed by warmth trickling down the back of my thigh.

"Daddy!"

"Be brave, Little Red. Almost done," he grits out.

My nails bite into my palms.

Then the head of his cock presses at my opening while the pain sears through me. He's using his knife to write something on my ass cheek, marking me, and I welcome it.

"Daddy's little whore looks delicious bleeding so beautifully for him."

I push back against the head of his cock when the pain forces me to bite into my lip, but he doesn't allow me to push far, holding me still so he can continue with the marking. "That's it. Take your pain out on me, Little Red.

Let Daddy's thick cock stretch you wide." I try not to wiggle my ass as his words send flurries of euphoria through me.

The knife clangs to the floor, and his strong hand grips my hip.

He grabs my hair and wraps it around his fist, yanking my head up to face the front of the chapel. "Now, pray for Daddy to fill you."

"Oh god," I whine as he torturously slides slowly inside me.

"Pray!"

"Please."

"More!" he barks.

"I promise to be good. Please fill me with your cock, Daddy."

"You're Daddy's whore, aren't you?" The feral tone in him has me wanting to comply. All his tenderness gone, his wildness unraveled into his savage self, and I wouldn't change him for the world. Instead, I embrace it. I welcome it with open arms, kneeling on an altar for my man.

"I'm your whore, Daddy. Please, I need it." I push back.

He spits on my ass, then shocks the hell out of me by slapping me hard on the marked flesh, and I cry out as he sinks inside me.

The pain mixed with pleasure is all-consuming, and my mind doesn't know which one to register first.

When he presses on my asshole with wet fingers, I see stars.

"Yes, Daddy. Yes."

"Fuck, Little Red. You look so good covered in my mark, so good covered in blood." His fingers pump deeper, and I have no choice but to clench his cock. I imagine him in all his glory, his head tipped back as his pleasure takes over him, and his lips parted as I scream his name.

The man is my god, and I willingly pray at his feet.

Chapter Thirty-Four

Rocco

I swallow back the lump in my throat as we turn into my father's estate. Nervousness is not a feeling I'm accustomed to, and truth be told, I've only ever felt it around Hallie.

She stirs beside me, her body spent after I fucked her brutally at the altar while marking her ass with my name.

"Little Red." I place the car into park and gently rouse her. "Hallie, wake up."

She startles awake and darts her head around, taking in my family's home. "Where are we?"

"At my dad's."

A choked noise leaves her lips. "I-I thought we would be going back to the cabin."

My lip twitches at her words. Knowing she loves the cabin so much has my veins filling with warmth. One day,

I hope to relocate my family there, if my father ever allows it.

"No, baby. We need to inform my father of our marriage."

A soft cry leaves her pouty lips, and I brush the stray hairs from her face. "Don't worry, Little Red. I've got you."

"Rocco, I don't think he's going to like this."

There's fear in her tone, and I can't help the chuckle that escapes me. "You're right. He's going to fucking hate it, but he doesn't have a choice."

Without giving her a chance to argue, I throw open the car door and make my way toward hers.

The sooner I deal with this shitshow, the better.

But one thing is for sure.

Hallie is a Marino now, and nothing he says will change that.

Hallie

A tremble racks through my body, causing me to grip Rocco's hand tighter. He glances at me over his shoulder and gives me a reassuring smile.

The house is magnificent, with marbled floors and chandeliers. Magnificent but cold. It lacks personal touch, as if it's all for show.

My heels click on the floor as we make our way toward a big wooden door. Rocco knocks once, then enters, pulling me in behind him.

"Where the fuck have you been?" Dark eyes rise from the computer and find mine, causing my breath to still. This man before me screams importance and oozes confidence. His white shirt is stretched taut over his shoulders, with his sleeves pulled up to his elbows, exposing his golden skin and thick veins. His silver hair is styled to the side, and the scent of his cologne hangs in the air. He's handsome and powerful, an older version of

Rocco, and the thought takes my breath away. His gaze scans over me before he flicks it back to his son's.

"You deaf?"

"Nah, I'm not old like you," Rocco jokes, then throws himself in a chair opposite his father. Pushing me in the one next to it, he quickly takes my hand in his. The mark on my ass makes me suppress a whimper, trying my best not to draw attention.

His father misses none of the actions and watches Rocco like a hawk. "What's this?" He waves his hand between us, and my mouth goes impossibly dry.

"This is my wife, Hallie."

Oh, sweet Jesus. Panic grips me as his father's eyes narrow on him. The muscles on his neck coil and his nostrils flare as he leans forward on his desk.

"Come again?"

Rocco shuffles from side to side and chuckles, but it lacks humor, exposing his nervousness, and I squeeze his hand to give him reassurance.

"I told you, you're going deaf." He juts his chin out. "I said she's my wife."

Rocco's father looks fit to burst, his face becomes redder by the second. "Oh, I heard you perfectly, you dumb little fucker. But you're engaged to the Harrington girl, so you can't possibly be married." I flinch at his mention of the engagement, and his eyes slice to mine before returning just as quickly to his son's.

Rocco holds my hand up, exposing my ring to his father, and I swear I could slide off my chair at his lack of tact.

DECEPTION

"We're married. Harrington is going to have to deal with it."

His father's nostrils flare wider, and he heaves in a breath before slowly exhaling. The atmosphere between us is filled with a tension that steals the air from my lungs while I wait for a reaction.

"There's been a contract in place for years, you know this." He slams his fist on the desk, causing his computer to rattle.

Rocco leans forward. "And I told you it wasn't going to happen." His voice is calm and collected, and something tells me he knows when to push his father and when not to.

"Fuck!" His father swipes the contents of his desk to the floor, and I cry out at his outburst. Before I know what I'm doing, I'm out of my chair, then Rocco leaps up and stands in front of me.

"Calm the fuck down, old man. You scare my girl and I'm going to put a fucking bullet in your head, Mafia don or not."

The air between us thickens as I wait for his father's reaction.

A loud laugh fills the room, followed by a heavy, defeated sigh.

Rocco steps aside, allowing me to see his father again. His father scrubs a hand over his head.

"My apologies, Hallie. My son has caused a fucking nightmare." He glares at Rocco with vengeance in his eyes, and a shudder flashes through me as I entwine my fingers with Rocco's again. He presses me under his arm and places a reassuring kiss on the top of my head.

"Why the hell do I think there's more to come from you?" His eyes drill into Rocco's, and my hand tightens in his. Again, his father's eyes flicker over our exchange before returning to his son.

He sure as hell misses nothing, and that thought has my stomach churning.

"It's complicated."

"Complicated?" he asks, dragging a finger over his top lip. "Sit and explain."

Rocco huffs, then takes a seat, but this time, he sits me on his lap. I wince at the bite of pain on my ass, then my cheeks flame with heat, knowing his father is scrutinizing us.

"Hallie is divorced." His father clucks his tongue, and Rocco ignores it, continuing on. "She, erm..." He shuffles and drags his hand through his hair.

"Spit it fucking out, Rocco, I have a date tonight," he bites out.

"Fine. Her son is my best friend."

"The Math's kid?" His father's eyebrows furrow.

"Right, Matt. But his father is an issue."

"Back the fuck up. Your ex-husband is an issue? This is why his panties are in a twist?" He looks to me, and I can only nod.

"Get rid of him." He shrugs at Rocco, and my spine straightens.

"I don't think that's a good idea." Rocco grimaces.

"Why the fuck not?" His bellow is loud, but I don't

DECEPTION

flinch. I'm becoming accustomed to this family's volatile behavior, yet somehow, I still feel safe.

"It's Gerrard Davis," Rocco all but whispers.

His father's jaw tics. "Speak up, it appears I'm a little deaf after all."

"I said, Gerrard fucking Davis, and you know it," Rocco snaps out, with fire in his eyes.

His father throws himself back in his chair and drags his hand down his face. "Fucking dumb little bastard." He shakes his head.

When he finally faces us again, his face is impassive, and my heart thuds erratically.

"I'd like to speak with Hallie." Rocco stiffens, and instantly, I want to reassure him. "Alone," he adds.

"No." Rocco's sharp response has his father's shoulders tightening, so he leans forward, his eyes promising punishment.

"It wasn't a question." The darkness in his tone makes my heartbeat faster, but not as fast as Rocco's, and I find myself wanting to protect him from his father's onslaught. It's the least I can do, knowing the predicament we're in.

"It's okay. I'm happy to speak with your father." I swallow back the nerves lingering in the pit of my stomach.

"No." Rocco doesn't so much as look at me, and it pisses me off. As much as it's nice to have him want to protect me, I've lived with a monster for years. In the past fifteen minutes of being in his father's office, I've come to learn his father doesn't like to terrify women, and the fact he apologized for scaring me proves as much. He might be deadly to men, but to me, he's all bark and no bite.

Rocco was telling the truth when he said his family doesn't hurt women and children, and that gives me the confidence I need.

"I said it's fine," I snap back at Rocco, and he turns to search my eyes. I lower my tone. "I've dealt with a classroom of unruly teenagers, Rocco. I can deal with your father."

His father releases a chuckle, and I realize he most certainly is not deaf.

"Your brother is waiting for you in his office," his father, whose name I've yet to learn, says.

Rocco scoffs and slips me from his lap, placing me on the chair, then he bends and places a kiss on my lips. "Shout for me if you need me."

"I won't," I state with a jut of my chin.

"That's my girl." He grins as he turns on his boots and heads toward the door.

Chapter Thirty-Five

Vinny

Sitting back in my chair, I watch the exchange between my son and his wife. I always knew when Rocco fell, it would be hard. I just hoped it would be for the Harrington girl.

Still, after witnessing their chemistry, I don't think I have much choice in the situation.

Of course, being the Mafia don means I have the power to force Rocco to give up his girl, but I refuse to do that, especially if what I'm suspecting is true.

The door clicks shut behind my son, and I turn my attention back to the little redhead who's trying her best to appear confident.

"You're pregnant."

She sucks in a sharp gasp, and her lip wobbles. The last thing I want to do is upset her, but I need the truth out of her, and quickly, if I'm about to go to war for my future grandchild.

"Is it Rocco's?"

Her mouth falls open, and her eyes widen. "Of course!" she snaps back. "How dare you!"

I chuckle at the fire behind her. Moments ago, she was a meek and mild weakling, and now she's a spitfire. I understand what Rocco sees in her, but thankfully, she's nothing like the blonde submissives I prefer; they'd never argue with me, for a start.

"He doesn't know," I state, and her shoulders slump.

I hadn't missed the way her hand was protecting her stomach when she was scared, but my son was too enthralled in protecting her to notice. I never miss a damn thing.

"He doesn't."

"Why?"

Her eyes glisten, but she fights back the tears.

"I think Gerrard is going to be an issue when he discovers the truth." She turns her head and blinks away her emotion before facing me again. "He will go insane if he discovers I'm pregnant, and I'm scared. I'm scared for Rocco, and I'm scared for this baby." Her hand rests on her stomach again.

"When Rocco married you, he was offering you our protection."

She nods, but I don't think she quite realizes the gravity of our protection.

"You need to tell him."

"I will."

DECEPTION

I stare into her hazel orbs. "Today."

"Yes, sir." Fuck me, she can't possibly know the implications of her words. I clear my throat and will my cock not to throb. I can't get hard for my son's wife. Fuck no.

I shake my head to rid myself of the thought. "You can call me Vinny." I hold my hand out to her, and when she slips hers in mine, I'm relieved when I don't have so much as a twitch of hunger toward her. "And don't worry about a damn thing. We will protect you, your son, and my grandchild, and my boy knows how to protect himself." I wink at her.

Then I press the button beneath my desk, and almost immediately, a knock arrives at the door. "Yes."

Mara, one of my maids, enters the room. "This is Rocco's wife, Hallie." Her eyes widen, then she curtsies toward Hallie. "Nice to meet you, ma'am." Hallie's cheeks pinken.

"Could you settle Hallie in Rocco's room while he finishes with Rafael?"

"Of course, Mr. Marino."

"Now go and tell Rocco the good news." I lift my chin to Hallie, and she smiles tightly.

"Thank you, and I'm truly sorry to cause you such trouble," she whispers, and heads toward the door.

I gift her with a smile I don't particularly feel. Deep in my soul, I know we're about to feel the wrath from numerous directions, and that leaves me with no choice but to pick up the phone and call in a favor.

"O'Connell, I need your assistance ..."

Chapter Thirty-Six

Rocco

I swing open the door to Rafael's office, and he sneers in my direction. "Have you any fucking idea what shit you left me in?"

"No. But I'm sure you're about to tell me." I settle into the chair opposite him.

"Warehouse four is gone."

"Gone?" I raise an eyebrow.

"Gone, burned to the fucking ground." He exhales loudly.

I sag back into the chair. "Shit."

"Exactly."

"I hope she's worth it." His eyes hold mine, and I nod. He releases a sigh. The poor bastard was forced into an arranged marriage with the devil woman he paid to stay out of his and his son's lives. I knew the moment he moved the teenage nanny in he would fall for her. What we didn't count on was her discovering Rafael's secrets that made her feel she had no choice but to run away. When he finally tracked her down, she'd given birth to his son.

"We're losing control, Rocco." I swallow hard at the deflation in his words. He's right, we're constantly being hit with FBI raids. Gerrard's younger brother Darryl set one of our clubs on fire as part of a setup that locked up Rafael, and now, I've added a whole new batch of problems to the mix, but I don't have it in me to regret any of it.

Not a single fucking thing.

"I have Owen from STORM Enterprises looking into the Davis family. They're corrupt as fuck, we know that. It's just proving it." I nod.

"How's Tommy doing?" I ask, desperate to change the subject before I incriminate myself further in the downfall of our family.

My older brother Tommy is an ex-addict. He's also obsessed with his young stepdaughter, so much so, she's already pregnant with their second baby despite just having the first.

Although, I never get the younger woman thing, I can't say I blame him. Given the chance to knock Hallie up in quick succession makes my cock ache with a need only she can satiate. The fact Hallie is all woman, curves and all, has my feet hitting the floor.

"Where are you going?"

DECEPTION

"I need to check on my girl."

"You only just got here."

"I'll be back in a few hours." I wink at him as I head toward the door, leaving behind a tirade of insults.

Chapter Thirty-Seven

Hallie

I spin in Rocco's room in shock. It's a pit. An actual pit. But worse than that, my face is plastered all over one wall like a shrine. The dresser leaning against the wall is covered in items I recognize. From lacy pink panties I misplaced months ago, to a coffee cup with my name on the side with my lipstick mark on the rim. There's a tub of my moisturizing lotion, a pillowcase, and small trinkets from my everyday life.

Some images I barely even remember where I was and what I was doing. They capture me in moments I assumed I was invisible to everyone.

"You were never invisible to me. From the first moment I saw you, you captured me, Little Red. It's you who stole me." His hand wraps around my throat, not a hint of threat in his action.

I hadn't realized I'd spoken aloud until he rephrased

my words. He owns all of me, even my thoughts. Maybe that's how he feels about me?

"You've been stalking me," I whisper, the accusation evident.

"You know this already." He places soft kisses down the side of my neck, tilting my head with one of his palms, and the heat of his touch is intoxicating as I sway on my feet, lost in his passion. Then he pulls back, gone as quick as he came. "Get naked on the bed, I want to show you something."

"Rocco, we need to talk."

He ignores me and begins undressing.

"Rocco, I've something to tell you."

"I want to show you something first." The excitement vibrates from him as he grabs the TV remote and nods toward the bed. Butterflies take float in my stomach as my mind flashes to him recording us having sex. The way I watched him come inside me while telling me he was filling me with his baby makes my core clench with arousal.

Still, I need to remain steadfast.

"Roc ..." He turns to face me, and his jaw locks tight. The glare he gives me has me sighing with a huff. I do as he asks and take a deep breath to lift the dress over my head, feeling gross that I haven't showered yet, and my ass is no doubt covered in my blood, along with the remnants of our cum.

"On your hands and knees."

"Seriously?" I glance at him over my shoulder but become transfixed at the way he pumps his thick cock. I

DECEPTION

didn't notice he pressed the remote until slaps of skin fill the room along with sounds of our combined pleasure. My gaze darts to faces on the television.

Without realizing, I find myself in the position Rocco asked for, and he positions himself behind me as wetness gathers, courtesy of the scene playing out on the big screen. Rocco is fucking me from behind, staring intently down at where we're connected. Much like now, and eagerness gathers at the thought.

"Do you see how good Daddy is fucking your little cunt?"

A breathy sob leaves me on screen, and I have no choice but to mirror it, the adrenaline rushing through me.

When Rocco slides his thick cock inside me, I mewl at the stretch despite being wet and ready for the taking.

His hips work quicker, and my pussy weeps with each withdrawal of his cock. "Watch this, Little Red." The screen cuts to him standing above me, jerking his cock over my face as I open my mouth to accept his cum.

I push back on his thickness, embracing the stretch. "Do you like watching Daddy play with you on the screen?"

"Yes, Daddy."

Slam.

"You like being Daddy's good little whore?"

Thrust.

"Yes."

"Do you like knowing I film us, Little Red? That we can watch ourselves get off on one another?"

My nipples graze his soft sheet with each powerful thrust, and I crave for him to suck them.

"Yes, Daddy."

"Do you like watching yourself get fucked by Daddy's big cock?"

Wetness coats him with each filthy word. "Yes, I like watching you fuck me."

The screen changes to my classroom, and I gasp.

"Look at you." He yanks my head up by my hair. "The innocent teacher letting her student fuck a baby into her." I clench around him. He has no idea how precise his words are, but he feels it. "You like that, huh?"

"Yes," I whine.

"Turn your head!" he barks, and his firm hold of my hair loosens to allow me to turn, then he leans over my back. "Open your mouth." I do as he asks, and he delivers a slow deluge of spittle onto my tongue. "Swallow me down like a good whore, Little Red." I swallow, then snap my eyes forward at the sound of his powerful hips moving the desk as he fucks me ruthlessly.

He surges inside me deeper than before, and a whoosh of air leaves me.

"You want your student to get you pregnant, don't you?"

I cling to the sheets to anchor me. "Yes."

"Of course you do. You want your student to fill you with a baby, don't you?"

"Yes, Daddy."

"You like watching us create our baby."

"Yes ..." My eyes roll when he presses on my clit with his thick finger.

"Watch yourself suck me." His thrusts become erratic, and I know he's getting close too.

My mouth waters when I watch the screen. The way his cock leaks pre-cum over my cheeks has me begging for him, and when he slaps my face with his thick cock, I cry out at the degradation behind it, pleading with him for more.

"Please, Daddy, I want to taste you."

"Fuck." He grunts loudly. "Fuck."

Then, after one final slam, he holds himself still as his warm cum hits my walls and sparks my orgasm.

"Daddy fills you so well, Little Red. So fucking well," he croons as I hit the mattress.

Rocco

I roll her onto her back, and her panting causes her heavy tits to sway, and I have an overwhelming urge to suckle on her swollen nipples. With my cock still stuffed inside her, I bend and take her peak into my mouth, sucking on it gently while I caress the swell of her tit. Her fingers find my hair as we become lost in the tenderness of the moment.

I want nothing more than to feed from her when she has our babies, but first, I need to ensure she becomes pregnant. Perhaps it's time we had further medical intervention.

"Rocco?" She's breathless as she speaks, and I delight in the fact she enjoys this as much as me, it turns her on for me to use her tits this way, and that only heightens my need to do it.

"Mm," I garble around her tit.

"I've something to tell you."

"Hm."

"I'm pregnant."

My entire body freezes as my mind plays catch-up with her words. "I'm pregnant," she repeats as I pop off her nipple to seek the truth behind her words.

Tears of hope glisten in her eyes, and I could swim in them, bathe in them forever as she delivers me the best news I could ever wish for.

"Are you sure?" I ask, choked with emotion.

"Yes."

My hand finds her stomach, and I rest my palm there. "Are you in there, little one?"

I slice my gaze back up to hers, and our eyes lock with a love so strong I'm rendered speechless.

"I think I'll be showing soon," she whispers.

My lip twitches. "You do?"

She bites into her lip. "I know I've put on weight. I think it's going to fill out soon; that's what happened with Matty."

She's referring to the softness around her middle, the part of her that gives her insecurities when she should have none.

My father once said that nothing can prepare you for the moment you're told you will become a father, and he wasn't wrong. He also told me to only do it with someone I wanted to be a mom to the child, not just a mother, having learned the hard way. Not one of us has grown up with a mother figure, and the disappointment I saw when he used to look at my nephew Oliver before Ellie came into his life reassured me he would support me in my

DECEPTION

decision not to marry the Harrington girl. He didn't want me to make the same mistake he made with Rafael, Tommy, Ricardo, and me. "Do-do you know how far along you are?"

"No. But I think it happened early on."

"How early?" I ask, raising my head to give her my full attention.

Her cheeks color as she glances away before looking back at me with guilt in her eyes. "I never took the Plan B."

"You didn't?" Shock hits me. Never in a million years did I expect her to say that, especially after collecting it from the pharmacy along with what she thought was the contraceptive pill.

"I don't know why. But I guess I always wanted to keep a part of you." Her admission makes my heart do a weird flutter I've never felt before. She's essentially admitting she was just as enthralled with me as I was her.

"You love me." I grin.

She laughs. "I doubt I was in love with you on the first night, Rocco."

"Hm. I think you were. You just didn't know it yet."

She shakes her head, and as much as I love to see this side of her, I have the gnawing sense of betrayal lingering in my stomach, and I hate it. "We need to speak with Matt."

She throws her head down on the pillow. "I know."

"And I want to get you seen by someone as soon as possible."

"Okay," she whispers.

"But first I need to do something."

She lifts her head to face me as I slowly withdraw out of her dripping pussy.

"What?"

"Daddy needs to fuck this ass, Little Red."

Chapter Thirty-Eight

Rocco

My cum leaks from her, and my mouth waters to taste myself dripping from her soft, wet pussy, but instead, I slide the head of my thick cock up and down her hole, coating it in our cum.

"Is it going to hurt?" Her pupils are blown, and I revel in the fact my girl likes pain with her pleasure.

"Yes, Little Red. Daddy is going to stretch your little asshole wide open. It's going to hurt." Her breath hitches, but she doesn't attempt to deter me, not that she'd be able to.

I glide the tip up and down her asshole, tormenting her. "Daddy," she pants.

"Beg me."

"Please."

I slap her pussy.

"Beg nicely."

"Please, Daddy."

"What do you want, Little Red?" I fist my cock over her exposed hole.

"I want you to stretch my ass with your thick cock." A flush travels down her cheeks and over her face.

"That's a good girl."

Then I guide my slicked cock head past her tight barrier, and the knuckles on her fists whiten as she grips the sheets while I slowly stretch her ass open.

"Fuck, Daddy. It hurts." She bites into her lip.

"Yeah, but Daddy's going to make it so fucking good." I grunt as the pleasure zips up my spine.

My eyes roam over her body. Knowing my baby is growing inside her has exhilaration flooding my bloodstream, and my pulse skitters. My palm finds her stomach as one hand remains on her open thighs, then I thrust forward hard, giving her no choice but to take it all.

"Ahhh." Her back arches off the bed. "Oh god."

"Fuck, that's it. Let Daddy inside this tight little ass."

Her head is tipped back, and her eyes are squeezed shut, pissing me off. "Hallie!" Her eyes shoot open. "Be a good girl and watch me fuck your ass."

"I-I ..."

I withdraw my cock to the tip. "Watch. Watch Daddy stretch you open, Little Red."

She rests up on her elbows and glances to the mirror before gifting me a shaky nod.

Then I slide back inside.

"Play with your nipples, Little Red. It will help you

feel good." She gasps when her fingers find the peaked tips. "Good girl." I love the way her tits bounce as I fuck her with a ruthless savagery and her puckered hole squeezes me.

"Fuck, look at you. Taking Daddy's cock in your ass."

"Yes!"

"Your tits are going to be so big for Daddy, Little Red."

"Yes."

"Filling with milk to feed him. Like a good mama."

"Yes, Daddy."

My thrusts become erratic with each filthy spill of my tongue as I imagine her tits leaking for me.

"I want to see the milk in your mouth, Daddy."

"Fuck, yes," I mutter as my balls draw up.

"Hold on to our baby while I fuck you hard, Little Red." Her hand meets mine, and we hold her softness as my cock pistons in and out of her with fervor.

"Fuck. Fuck."

"Oh god, I'm coming. I'm coming, Daddy." Her body stiffens around me, and I've no choice but to give in.

I explode. A thousand white stars dance before my eyes as my cock unloads inside her. All her holes are mine, all of her belongs to me.

And nobody will take them from me.

Chapter Thirty-Nine

Hallie

We spent three days at Vinny's home, getting to know Rocco's family, and it has been both chaotic and eye-opening.

To begin with, the security surrounding the home was disturbing, but I became accustomed to it, and a sense of ease rippled through me at knowing how safe I was. How safe our baby is.

We make our way toward the private prenatal clinic, with Silas following in an SUV behind us. Rocco rolled his eyes when his father insisted on us no longer leaving the premises without security, but I couldn't help but feel thankful for the added protection bestowed upon us.

"We'll go straight to your house after and meet Matt there." Rocco eyes me from the corner of his eye before glancing back at the road.

"Okay." I chew on my lip as anxiety courses through

me. Today is a big day. We tell Matty about us and also check to make sure everything is okay with the baby, something I've been putting off doing.

"Don't worry, Little Red. It's all going to be okay."

I exhale as sickness rolls in my stomach. "He's going to hate me more than he does already."

Pulling into a parking space, he slams on the brakes, then winces at the jolt. He clears his throat. "I'm sorry." He lifts my chin and turns me to face him. "Matt doesn't hate you, and he won't."

I take a deep breath. He doesn't know my son like I do. His friendship with Rocco came when he needed him the most, not long after me and Gerrard split. The timing was perfect, and now he will feel like it was all a lie. After everything he's sacrificed to help make me happy, he will feel like I betrayed him.

"You'll see." He winks, then kisses my fingers with a confidence I don't feel. "Come on, let's go see baby Marino."

I chuckle at his enthusiasm and wait for him to get out and open my door for me. Something he explained he loved doing and was also for security reasons, and who am I to argue with that?

If there's something I've learned while being in the Marino family, it's that they value women and children, and with that thought in mind, I slip my hand into Rocco's and step into our future.

Rocco

My mind feels foggy as a haze of fury washes over me. "You want to touch her stomach? You do realize that's my wife, right?" I point to Hallie's startled face on the hospital bed.

"Sir, we need to examine her." The ponce in the white jacket tries to reason with me, but I scoff as I glare at the little prick. He just wants a reason to touch what doesn't belong to him.

When Rafael gave me the best obstetrician in the area's phone number, it definitely said Mrs. in front of it. "I asked for the best, not some jumped up little punk wanting to cop a feel."

"Rocco!" Hallie snaps, but I ignore her.

"Sir, as I previously explained, Mrs. Hartley is sick today with the flu. I'm her stand in, and my credentials are just as impressive." He lifts his chin as if proud of himself. Well, woo hoo for him. Not a fucking chance.

"So you fucking say," I grit out.

"Can you just let him do his job?" Hallie's gaze darts from mine to his, and I want to demand her to only look at me, but I thrust my hand in my pocket in an attempt to not pull the knife my fingers itch to use.

"We need to check the baby, sir. With Mrs. Marino unsure how far along she is, it's vital we check her thoroughly."

A strangled choke lodges in my throat. "Thoroughly?"

"Sir, I will place the transducer on her stomach, and it will generate the echo to the monitor." He points toward the screen. "I just need to lube her up first."

My temper skyrockets. "Lube. Her. Fucking. Up?" Each word sounds deadlier than the last. Just who the hell does this chump think he is?

He holds his hands up. "Sir. Mrs. Marino may have been taking medication during the gestation of her pregnancy, and I want to ensure nothing has hindered the development of the baby."

My spine straightens and a slice of pain lances through my chest, making it difficult for me to breathe. The thought that I might have caused harm to my unborn child is crippling.

"Sleeping tablets. She's taken sleeping pills." I trip over my words, desperate to get them out.

"Rocco, I haven't." She shakes her head.

"She's had sleeping pills," I say, more firmly as Hallie's eyes bore into me.

"Okay, well, I don't think that would be an issue, but

DECEPTION

we need to look at her to be sure." The tension in my body falls at his words.

I cross my arms over my chest and widen my stance. "I'll lube her up. You can wait outside while I do."

His mouth opens to speak, and I glare at him, then he clears his fat throat and nods. "Very well, sir. Let me know when you're ready."

Chapter Forty

Rocco

As soon as the door closes behind him, I spin to face Hallie's death glare. Choosing to ignore it, I lift my T-shirt I insisted on her wearing to the appointment, another way to stake my claim.

"Sleeping pills? How do I not know about this?"

"Because you were asleep, Little Red," I say with a cocky smile as I unzip my jeans.

Her eyes dart around the room before landing back on me. "Rocco, what the hell are you doing?"

I hiss when my palm makes contact with my solid cock. I've been rock hard since discovering she's pregnant, and it shows no sign of going down despite fucking her multiple times a day.

"Giving you lube."

Her mouth falls open, and I can't help myself as step

forward and position myself at her lips. "Lick it for Daddy."

Heat travels over her cheeks, and I imagine it covering her glorious tits too. Then her little tongue darts out and licks over my swollen head, and I grunt in pleasure when her tongue dips into the slit. "Spit on me, Little Red. Spit on your daddy. Give me lube too."

Her breathy whimper has my balls aching, and when her spittle lands on the head of my cock, I revel in the degradation of it. Fuck me, that's hot.

"Such a slut for Daddy."

Without me prompting her, she sucks on the head of my cock; the vibrations of her moans send liquid fire shooting through my body as I race toward my orgasm.

I palm her stomach and close my eyes—fucking bliss. "My wife pregnant with my baby, sucking my cock on a hospital bed like a greedy whore." I roar with a thrust of my hips. "Gonna come all over you, Little Red. Gonna paint you in Daddy's cum. Going to lube you up."

"Play with your tits. Play with those big tits for me." A string of saliva leaves her lips as she pops off my cock to pull the T-shirt above her tits. I slap my cock on her cheek. "Suck it," I grit out, hating that she detached herself from me.

The sight of her tits about to burst from her bra has my fist working faster, and when she massages them seductively while swallowing me down, I have no choice but to bite my cheek in a hope to stave off my orgasm.

Her tongue works down my shaft and back up, then

DECEPTION

she sucks on my head like her life depends on it, drawing my cum out of me at a rapid pace.

"Fuck."

I tug her off my cock and aim it at her stomach. "Fuck." I buck my hips as I fire my cum over her softness, marking what belongs to me.

"Mine."

Hallie

I lie back in shock. That did not just happen ...

My heavy pants fill the room, my head swimming with the possession radiating from him. He zips up his jeans and stares down at his handiwork, and part of me wants to wipe it away. He's insane, feral, a savage, and I crave it. What does that make me?

He tugs my T-shirt to below my bra, covering me while my head swims in a haze as I lie there stupefied. Then he opens the door and whistles. Fucking whistles.

Slapping a hand over my face, I whine at his antics.

The doctor returns and takes one look at my stomach before turning a deep shade of red. I glance away and up toward Rocco, who stands towering over the doctor with his arms folded across his chest and a smug, cocky grin on his face.

Jesus. I rub at the pressure point on my temple.

"You good?" Rocco's voice cuts through the fog.

"A little headache."

He nods. "You need a release, Little Red. I'll give you one. Let him do his job first." He tilts his head toward the doctor, who scrambles to set up the scanner while my mouth falls slack at his blatant insinuation.

Rocco pulls up a chair and takes my hand in his. His thick fingers play with my wedding ring, and my heart warms at the motion. All the embarrassment and anger I feel toward him leaves with the simple action.

When the scanner makes contact with my stomach, I flinch, and Rocco growls toward the doctor. "You hurt my woman, and I'll cut your fucking hands off and force you to eat them, understand?"

I can't help the laugh that bubbles up inside me at his words. Then I search his face, and it promises retribution. Holy shit, he's serious.

"Ye-yes, sir." The doctor's hand trembles, and I want to tell him not to worry, but a soft whirling sound fills the room, then Rocco stills and turns his head to face the computer screen.

"There we go." The doctor points toward the little blob on the screen, and my heart swells at the sight. Several clicks occur while Rocco and I remain transfixed.

"We did it, Little Red. We made a baby." His tone is filled with awe, and that alone has emotion erupting inside me. "It's incredible," he whispers.

"Everything looks good. Little one appears to be almost twenty weeks."

"That's nearly five months, right?"

"That's correct," the doctor confirms.

A wide grin spreads across Rocco's face, and he

brings my hand to his lips, kissing them gently. "We were fucking meant to be, Little Red."

A lump catches in my throat, and I can only nod in response.

"Would you like to know the sex?"

Rocco's eyebrows shoot up, and he sits forward to stare at the screen. "You can tell?"

"Yes, sir. Mr. Marino, sir." The doctor stumbles over his words, and I chew on my lip to refrain from laughing.

Rocco tilts his head to face me. "You want to know?"

"You choose," I whisper.

The moment I say the words, excitement buzzes through him. His eyes dance and his body practically vibrates as I wait to hear what we're having.

He turns to the doctor. "Go ahead and tell us."

"A girl, sir. Erm, Mr. and Mrs. Marino, congratulations, you're having a girl."

"A little girl." Rocco's entire face lights up. "We're having a baby girl, Hal."

And all I can do is nod. The love in his eyes as his gaze flicks back and forth from me to the computer screen is like nothing I have ever witnessed before.

Rocco Marino may be a deranged savage, but he's completely in love with me and our baby, and that makes us the most powerful couple in New Jersey.

Chapter Forty-One

Rocco

A daughter. I'm having a daughter with the most beautiful woman on the planet. I bet she'll have red hair like her mama. Little freckles over her nose like her too.

Once the doc finished measurements and other shit I knew nothing about, he told us all was good, then took blood samples and rebooked us in for another appointment for in a month's time with the female doctor.

I text my father to tell him the good news, and he replied with a thumbs-up. Fucking prick. The least the old bastard could do was give me a pink heart or something for his granddaughter.

As soon as Hallie can get pregnant again, I'll do it. I already love her pregnant body more than I thought I would. I imagine my need for her will only increase the bigger she gets, and those tits—fuck me. When her milk comes in, I'll be bathing in it.

I wonder if that's possible.

"You're nervous too, aren't you? That's why you're fidgeting." I slice my eyes to hers, then back to the road and try my hardest to suppress the insane laughter begging to escape. She really thinks I'm nervous to tell Matt? Jesus, it'll be a relief to finally get it all out. And fidgeting? My cock is rubbing on the waistband of my denim and hurts like a bitch, but the way she's gnawing on her nails tells me she isn't going to appreciate my honesty. Still, I can't lie to her.

"He'll understand," I grunt noncommittedly.

We pull into her driveway, and I purposely park behind Matt's car, blocking the little runt in just in case he plans on making a quick exit and this doesn't go how I hope.

Before I give her a chance to overthink it, I'm out of the SUV and rounding her side to help her from the car. I give Silas a chin lift as her hand slips into mine. He rolls his eyes, unimpressed with having to become our shadow twenty-four seven.

When we step into her kitchen, she attempts to slip her hand from mine, but I only tighten my hold on her further. No fucking way is she pulling away from me.

"Hey, Mom." Matt sticks his head around the wall from the kitchen, then his eyes land on me. "Hey, man, what are you doing here?" He shakes his head. "Forget that. Roc, you can't be here, man. My dad—" He grinds his jaw as if pissed.

DECEPTION

"We need to talk to you," Hallie blurts.

"Oh, okay." When he steps out of the kitchen, his gaze lands on our connected hands, and again, Hallie attempts to pull away from me, but I tighten my hold. His eyes narrow and his jaw sharpens. "What's happening?" He stares at our hands as the room fills with tension. Hell, I can practically feel the anger building inside him as his chest rises and reality sets in.

Hallie opens her mouth, but I decide to explain for her. "We're married."

He chokes on a comical laugh and rocks back on his feet. Then his gaze locks back on us and all humor has faded. "Wh-what?"

"Married. Me and your mom." I lift our joined hands to show him her ring, and Hallie grinds her teeth while boring her eyes into the side of my head, but I ignore her. "And we're ..."

"Rocco, don't you dare!" She butts in, shaking her head.

"Pregnant." Her mouth falls open as I lay it all out for him. "Your mom and I are married, and she's having our baby." His face pales as his eyes flick from Hallie to mine, then back to Hallie's. Then he glances down at her stomach.

"You can't be," he whispers, forcing a strangled sob from Hallie.

"It wasn't planned." She attempts to pacify him, but I scoff. Wasn't fucking planned? Our little girl was most definitely planned, even if she wasn't always aware of it.

"He's my best friend," Matt murmurs. The brokenness of his tone actually makes my heart ache, but I choose to ignore it.

"Well, now I'm your best friend and your stepdad." I grin back at him.

"Rocco!" Hallie snaps. "You're not helping."

"He ... he's, barely two years older than me. What the fuck, Mom!" he bellows, and Hallie flinches.

I step forward, pissed he's shouting at her. "Lower your fucking tone, Matt," I grit out.

His eyes widen. "Lower my tone? You knocked my mom up and married her! Are you insane?"

"Yes." I smile broadly. "Very insane. But she's my sanity." I point toward Hallie. "That woman right there is the only reason I hold on to the little sanity I have, so I suggest you shut the fuck up and deal with it."

"Deal with it?" he sneers, shocking the shit out of me. Where the hell has the meek and mild Matt disappeared to. "If you seriously think I'm going to be okay with this, then you're deluded," he spits out, his tone now poisonous.

"Matt, please," she implores. "Can we just talk about it?"

"Dad is going to flip his fucking shit." He turns to me. "He hates you; you know that, right?"

When I shrug, all the anger drains from his face, as if realizing something. "You did this on purpose."

I cross my arms over my chest and lift my chin, unprepared to deliver him with my truths, not when Hallie isn't aware.

DECEPTION

"What the hell is this? Some revenge plot or something?"

"Don't be so fucking stupid. I love her," I snap back, pissed at his attitude.

"Love?" He laughs, and it's malicious. "You?" Then he spins to face Hallie, and I already know I won't like what he's about to say. I wait for the onslaught of vitriol to spill from him while every muscle in my body struggles to remain in control. "You stupid bitch. I hate ..." I move so fast I don't realize what I'm doing until Hallie cries and I'm staring down at Matt on the floor as I grip his T-shirt in my hand, my fist almost at his face.

"Rocco, how could you?" She sobs as she stares up at me. "Yo-you almost hit him." Her chin wobbles, and the disappointment in her tone forces me to step back. "You almost hit my son."

"I was protecting you," I fire back. I stopped myself and I'd never hurt either of them.

Her eyes turn from pitiful to angry in the blink of an eye. "Get out!" She points toward the door. "Get the fuck out!"

"No."

"I said get out, right fucking now, Rocco."

I stay grounded to the spot.

"Do you want me to ring the police?" She lifts her eyebrow, and I glare back at her. She knows damn well the hell that will rain down on us if that happens, all of us.

I drag my hand over my chin, trying but failing to find

a solution. "Fuck!" I march toward the door and throw it open.

How can she not see I was protecting her?

I slam the door behind me and storm toward the SUV.

Silas is at my side in a flash. "What happened?"

"I almost hit the kid." I drag a hand over my hair and tug it. "Shit!"

"Fuck, man. She went mama bear on you, huh?"

I slam my fist into the window screen and welcome the bite of pain, but this is nothing compared to how I feel inside, and however much I know Hallie did what's right by asking me to leave, I also know I'm not going anywhere. I'll just deal with the consequences the way I know best.

I'll take what I want, and she'll thank me for it.

Chapter Forty-Two

Hallie

I cried myself to sleep, unable to get my head around the fact my life is such a mess. My son is hurt because of me and my choices, and yet, no matter how much I hate that, I wouldn't change it for the world.

From the first night I had with Rocco, there was a connection, something beneath those dark eyes of his had me hooked. Maybe it was the softness that felt reserved solely for me, maybe it was his touch that ignited flames I never knew existed, or maybe it was the way his eyes devoured me, owned my body, and stole my heart with his need to protect and keep me.

I know he acted on instinct and almost hit Matt due to his poor choice of words. My son has never spoken to me that way before, and I doubt he will speak to me that way again. He couldn't apologize enough when Rocco left, and it broke my heart hearing those apologies. He's nothing like Gerrard, and the fact he felt like he was for speaking to me like that reiterated how different they are.

Matty is a soft soul with a gentle heart. It's another reason I left Gerrard. I didn't want his masochistic and poisonous tongue depicting such a vile representation as to how men should treat women.

When I held him close to my chest as we cried together, I told him I was sorry. The disappointment in his eyes had me second-guessing my entire future, but I remained steadfast for the sake of my baby. When he told me he needed space, my heart broke into a thousand pieces. I didn't just lose my son, but I lost my husband too.

Then I showered, hoping to wash away the feeling of guilt, and crawled into bed to let the tears fall into the pillow until I couldn't cry anymore.

I roll onto my side and become acutely aware of someone in the room. My heart catches in my throat as his scent filters through my bloodstream. He's here, and only now am I realizing he's done this before.

How many nights has he done this? Crept into my room and left me with trepidation in my veins while I remained disorientated and paranoid.

His words from the doctor's office come back to haunt me like pieces of a puzzle I'm only now stupidly putting together.

"She had sleeping pills." Did he drug me to watch me sleep? Or did he do more?

Images flash in my mind at all the positions he recorded us in. Some I don't remember being in. The items in his bedroom tell me Rocco has been obsessed with me far longer than I was ever truly aware.

"You drugged me," I whisper as I open my eyes and latch onto him in the chair in the corner of the room. His broad legs spread wide, his signature knife lies on his thick thigh, and his white T-shirt stretches over his shoulders. His eyes trail up to mine, and there's an edge to them, one I know all too well, one that has wetness gathering between my legs as my nipples peak, begging for his touch.

"I did," he confirms, with not one ounce of regret in his tone. "I wanted you compliant and full of my baby."

I sit up and the sheets pool at my waist, exposing my tits to him, just the way he likes.

He licks his lips like a predator full of hunger and promise.

A breathy, desperate sound leaves me, which is crazy, considering he just admitted to drugging me, but my body responds with desire. "What else did you do?"

The lengths he's gone to should terrify me, but instead, they ignite a spark inside me, bursting to explode.

"I jerk off in your lotion so you cover yourself in me every day."

My fingers find my clit while the other moves to my nipple, caressing the peak into a stiff bud, ready for him to suck on.

Jesus, I whine at his admission. "What else?" Knowing I use the lotion daily to coat myself in his essence has my veins pumping with gratification. He's completely feral, and only I can control him.

"I steal your worn panties and lick them while I fuck my hand."

I stroke over my aching clit. "Oh god."

"Show me," he whispers, and I drag the sheet from my waist and widen my thick legs to expose myself to him.

"Fuck," he growls.

I will him to pull his hard cock from his jeans to show me what I do to him too.

"More," I whisper as I slide two fingers into my hole, coating them in my slickness.

"I laid under your bed, jerking off when you were in the room." My hands work faster as I imagine him lying there, getting off on our proximity. "I fucked you while filming it, filled you with my cum while you were out cold, then licked my cum out of your dripping pussy so you wouldn't feel it leak from you."

"Oh god, Daddy."

"I painted your nipples in my cum, imagining it was milk coming from you."

My back arches as I tweak my nipple, and my orgasm hits while his words ring out in my ears. "I fucked my baby into you, whether you wanted me to or not." My breathing becomes rugged.

"I'm the shadow in the night, the demon beneath the bed, and I'm the monster who takes what he wants, consequences be damned."

He disrobes, and his footsteps play out like background noise. When he pushes me onto my back and his heaviness settles on top of me, I buck beneath him, but he doesn't move.

As his forehead rests against mine, love seeps from his eyes. "I'm completely insane. I've deceived you to get what I want. I'm obsessed. I'm a savage. But I'm yours, Hallie. Whether you like it or not, you own me. Don't ever push me away again, Little Red, because I'm not going anywhere."

Rocco

Watching my little red get off on my depravity is like a drug hitting my veins. If she thought I was obsessed before, that's nothing compared to now.

She may not have realized it, but she opened up a damn can of worms into my world of twisted morals. Of course, I need to consider her pregnancy, but that won't stop me from coming on her steering wheel so I know the last thing she touches before entering school will be my essence. Nor will it stop me from feeding from her glorious tits every chance I get.

"You're mine." Her words flutter over my face and fill me with the reassurance I yearn for from her. My lips find hers, and our tongues dance gently together, a stark contrast to the way I feel inside. When I pull back, her pupils are blown and her eyelids heavy.

She swallows hard. "Daddy, I need you to fill me."

My cock jerks. "Do you want Daddy to play nice? Or do you want me to treat you like a naughty slut?"

Her hips rise off the bed as I pin her down with my weight.

When her fingers tangle in my hair, I revel in delight, loving the way her touch sends a shiver of longing through me. The need to suckle on her tit has my cock leaking and my slit dripping pre-cum.

"I've been bad."

"Fuck, yes you have." I hiss as I grind my hips into her. "So, fucking bad, Little Red." I slide my cock inside her and relish the stretch of her pussy to accommodate me.

"That's it, Little Red, stretch around Daddy."

She releases a soft squeak at my words.

"Open your mouth."

She parts her lips, and I gather spittle in my mouth, then hover my face above hers and slowly spit onto her waiting tongue. Seeing her greedy and desperate mouth filled with me has me withdrawing from her slick pussy, and instead, I straddle her waist, careful not to rest on her stomach.

"Push your tits together." She moves quickly, and my cock jumps at the way her heavy tits allow the perfect cushioning for my cock to slide through. "My cock is dripping with your cunt juice." Aiming my cock at her nipples, I coat them in my pre-cum, then spit on them too, eager to have them wet and dripping for me, like her milk will.

Fuck, I can't wait for that.

My hips work faster and faster, and hers meet mine like for like as sweat coats my forehead.

DECEPTION

Then I slide my cock between her tits and slowly move. "Keep your mouth open and your tongue out, I'm going to cover your face with my cum, Little Red."

I grab the headboard above her, and fuck her tits faster and faster, and when my balls draw up, I stare down at my girl. "Good Little Red gets to eat my cum. Bad Little Red gets covered in it."

I slide through her once again, and my lips part in ecstasy as my hot cum splashes on her face, over her tongue, and down her delicate lips. My movements slow, but I don't stop, determined to cover as much of her as I can. "Fuckkk," I grind out.

"Such a pretty mess, Little Red. Let Daddy clean you up."

Next, I shuffle down her body, mindful of my baby growing inside her. I slide my cock into her waiting pussy while my tongue scoops my cum from her cheeks to deliver it to her mouth. When her fingernails bite into my jaw and she holds me in place to suck it from my tongue, I thrust deep inside her, the depravity of our actions sending me feral with need.

My hand finds her ass cheek, and I hold on to it as she pulls her legs up high in order for me to stare down at my cock sinking deep inside her.

Two star-crossed lovers embracing their depraved sins.

A union forged in deception.

Chapter Forty-Three

Hallie

Rocco held me all night despite his phone ringing and his messages pinging. He never paid it a bit of notice. His attention was solely on me, like nothing else existed, and that's how I feel when I'm with him. Like I'm the only person who matters.

He lifts his head from my nipple, and I feel the loss instantly. "You stopped stroking my hair. What's wrong?" His wet lips have me shuffling to ward off my desire for him.

I chew on my bottom lip.

He sits up. "Matt will come around, Hal, I promise."

I shake my head. "He's devastated."

A chuckle leaves Rocco. "Then he needs to man up."

My mouth drops open. "What?" How the hell can he be so heartless?

"Little Red. Devastated is seeing your favorite nanny have her brains blown out because she was fucking your older brother as well as you. The same nanny who was fucking your father."

Horror strikes me in the chest as I stare back at him.

"Devastated is knowing your mom never wanted you at all and instead took a paycheck that was pittance just to get away from you, then died anyway."

My heart constricts.

"Devastated is having your family labrador—"

I hold my hand up. "I get the point."

"Matt isn't devastated. He's acting out and being a dick. He'll come round."

"I hope so."

He moves from between my legs, and his cock stands tall and thick, and not for the first time, I wonder if there's something wrong with it. How the hell does it stay like that all the time?

"Where are you going?"

Glancing over his shoulder, he heads toward the door. "Getting my baby mama breakfast. Fresh smoothie and muesli, right?"

"Right," I confirm with a smile. As the door closes, I glance around the room, wondering where the cameras are that allow Rocco to know my every move. With a smile, I shake my head.

The man is certifiable for sure. But what the hell does that say about me?

Rocco

I glance from one brother to the other. When Rafael called this meeting, I knew we would be discussing the problems I've brought down on the family.

"Papa reached out to the O'Connell's." Tommy glares in my direction. He hates being indebted to anyone, but fuck him, we've kept this family going in his absence while he got to tap out and play poor me in rehab.

"We also have the added issue of the Harrington girl," Rafael states while staring above my shoulder. "I have a plan for that one."

Tommy sits forward with intrigue, but not me. I couldn't give a shit what they do with her or how they handle the situation.

"It's about time Ricardo stepped up."

My mouth falls open with Tommy's.

"You know where he is, then?" my dumbass brother asks Rafael.

"Of course I fucking know, and it's about damn time he paid for being absent all these years," Rafael snaps.

"You're going to get him to leave the MC?" I ask, knowing my brother won't like this, not one bit.

"I'm going to give him no choice but to marry a Mafia girl. Should he choose to be a part of the MC while being her husband, that's on him. But he will fulfill his duties, once and for all." The confidence in Rafael's tone has me certain our father signed off on this plan, and I should feel bad for putting Ricardo in this situation, but like Rafael said, he's been absent from his duties for years. Why shouldn't he finally be forced to step up?

"So, you're going to be a daddy?" Tommy grins, changing the subject and causing me to mirror his smile with pride.

"Sure am."

"Welcome to the club, brother." He holds his fist out for me to bump, and I take great delight in participating.

Rafael clears his throat. "If we can stay on fucking topic."

Tommy huffs and sits back in his chair.

I won't lie, being in the same room with my brothers, working together as a collected trio, has me feeling more invincible than ever. Now we need a plan to back it up.

"I say we take off the head of the snake and work our way down." I drag the tip of my knife down my tongue, and I swear I can still taste the juice of Hallie's pussy on the blade.

"No. We're not in a position to take down the chief of

police, dumbass," Rafael says. "But we do need to make a statement."

I sit forward. "What did you have in mind?"

Rafael sits forward with a smile. "The kid." He's referring to Gerrard's younger brother, the same one who set Oblivion on fire, no doubt believing we wouldn't retaliate because he's deemed untouchable. "We make him pay." Of course, Rafael still has a vendetta toward him. He tried to snag his girl, after all, so who could blame him.

"That would be too obvious and put us under too much scrutiny. They must know by now we're diverting shipments. If the O'Connell's get dragged into this for helping us out, then we lose reliable allies."

Tommy's right.

"I could take off his hands. That's a pretty big fucking statement to not to touch what's ours." I shrug.

Rafael pinches the bridge of his nose and tips his head toward the ceiling.

The door to his office is thrown open, and we all turn to glare toward the bastard who dared to intrude without permission.

A cumulative sigh comes from us all when our father walks into the room.

I'll give the man his dues; he exudes power and commands attention simply by striding into a room.

He pulls out his chair at the head of the table, and Rafael clenches his teeth. He's desperate to take over our family completely, and in all honesty, he'd be good at it.

The thing is, our father doesn't want to give it up, not yet anyway.

"Don't you have a cute little sub somewhere you can play with?" Rafael sneers toward him, the distaste evident in his tone.

Our father has made no effort to disguise his sexual preferences. Since being a young boy, I've known he's a dominant who parades his submissives around our house as if it's normal. For us, it was, but that's not what I want for my kids.

I like the quiet life in Hallie's little house, a little family shielded from all this Mafia shit. Until I'm needed, of course, then I will do what is asked of me.

"I received a phone call."

A laugh bubbles out of me, and I can't help the sarcasm as it spills out. "Well done, old man. Did you need to remember to switch your hearing aid on this time before you pressed the answer button?"

Before I know what's happening, my Adam's apple is being squeezed so fucking tight I can't breathe, and it feels like I'm being stabbed in the throat.

"Jesus fucking Christ," Rafael bellows. "Papa, enough!" He slams his fist on the table.

He drops me back into my chair, and I gasp for air, each breath burning, and I grimace as my hand strokes over my delicate throat.

"Now you know how a woman's throat feels when you throat-fuck her." Tommy chuckles into my ear, and I glare back at him. His lips tip up into a smile, and I want to slice the motherfucker for it.

DECEPTION

"It's your fucking fault we have the FBI breathing down our goddamn neck!" He points in my direction, his lips twisted in hatred. "How dare you fucking joke! You little sad sack son of a bitch."

Okay, maybe I took it too far too soon.

My extra-curricular activities are still recent and raw.

I open my mouth to speak, but he holds his hand up. "Shut the fuck up. I don't want to hear it."

It's on the tip of my tongue to tell him he probably wouldn't be able to hear it, but I decide not to push my luck. It might be my balls he tries to squeeze out of me next, and I need those fuckers as much as I need air, especially with the number of kids I plan on impregnating Hallie with.

"As I was fucking saying. I had a phone call; Owen from STORM Enterprises contacted me." Rafael sits forward. He's worked with this Owen guy before. "It appears he has information on Harrison Davis being into human trafficking."

Nausea hits me, and I fight back the bile creeping up my throat. The thought of Matt and Hallie being a part of that sick family sends a tremor of fear down my spine. They're far more dangerous than I could have ever predicted, which means they've been in danger for a long time, and I hate myself for not acting sooner.

Tommy whistles like the cat that got the cream, sitting back in his chair with a smug smile.

Rafael's jaw falls slack, and he scans our father's face. "Human trafficking? The chief of police? Is he sure?"

"He's watched the footage," he states with a confident nod.

"Does he still have it?" I hear the hope in Rafael's voice and feel it in my veins.

"No."

"Fuck," I grunt, then immediately wince at the tenderness behind it.

"You sound like your balls have just dropped," Tommy mumbles into my ear, and my fingers itch to take my knife to him.

"How does he know Harrison wasn't just undercover?" Rafael asks.

"He assures me he wasn't. So much so, he's willing to help us take him down."

Holy shit. I want to say it but opt not to, preferring to save my voice for Hallie.

"What about Gerrard?" Tommy asks, and I want to high-five my brother for thinking of my predicament.

"We need surveillance on them. That Darryl kid too, all three of them." My father's voice is assertive, as if he's already thought of this before informing us of this news.

"You think the kid's involved?" Rafael asks, his eyebrows pull together.

"At this stage, we treat them as if they're all involved. Until they prove otherwise." I nod.

Sickness rolls in my stomach at the thoughts of the sick bastards around my family portraying a normal family life when they're anything but normal. I might be a monster, but I'd never hurt women and children. These sick fucks are a different breed entirely.

DECEPTION

Human fucking trafficking? Jesus. I scrub a hand over my face. "I don't like the thought of Matt around them."

"And Hallie," Tommy tacks on.

I scoff, then end up choking, which hurts like a bitch even more. "She isn't going anywhere near him again. Ever." I stare back at my brother, and he smirks, knowing how much I mean it.

"Is Hallie on lockdown?" Rafael asks. As much as I'd like to say yes, I know how much her career means to her. Ideally, I'd still be a student there, but I don't want to break my promise with her. Besides, she's going to be showing off a wedding ring and baby bump, and the last thing my girl needs is for people to be digging deeper into her private life.

"No. She still wants to work; I'll ask Matt to look out for her while she's there and have Silas take her to and from school."

"I don't like the thought of my grandbaby being so out of reach," my father states while swiping his finger over his lip, and for the first time since announcing my union with Hallie, he shows concern for my little family, and the thought warms me.

I shuffle from side to side as anxiety creeps up my spine. "Me neither." I shrug.

"Are you moving her into one of my properties?" he asks, and I sit forward, preparing for his argument.

"No. I have her house so tapped and wired there's more security on that street than a prison."

"Does she know you own the street yet?" Tommy grins.

"No," I snap back. How the hell will I explain that to her?

"Does she at least know you own the house?" Rafael asks.

I lick my lips, and even that somehow hurts my throat. "Not yet."

"Think you should tell her?" he asks.

"I think you should keep your nose out of my goddamn business."

"It's your fucking business that put us in this situation," he snipes.

"Pretty fucking sure your girl was caught with her tongue down the Davis kid's throat and you roughed him up. That probably started a chain of events too." I shrug.

Tommy laughs, and Rafael looks two seconds away from blowing a gasket.

My father slams his fist down on the table. "Shut the fuck up! Both of you. Rocco, keep your woman and baby close to you. The kid too. If he's gonna be part of this family, I want his loyalty."

I swallow back the painful lump in my throat at the thought of my father accepting Matt into our family, especially given his family are descendants of the criminal justice system. "You can trust him," I say with confidence.

I know Matt. I've spent the last two years getting close to that kid, so I know him. Probably better than he knows himself. He's my best friend.

He's loyal.

Strong.

Dependable.

And most importantly, he's my stepson, and there isn't a damn thing I wouldn't do to protect him.

Rocco

Two years ago …

Matt stares down at the floor, toeing his sneaker into the ground. "I'm, like, three feet shorter than you." He chuckles, and I smirk at his assessment. To be fair, he's not far off. I am six foot two.

"You'll grow." I shrug.

"I'm not like you." Vulnerability flashes in his eyes, and I hate it. Staring back at me are the same hazel eyes I adore, minus the green specks that make hers even more unique.

"You have other strengths."

"Like what?"

"You can run."

He scoffs. "Run from the bullies." He shakes his head. "That's not what I want." He broadens his shoulders, and I see the truth behind his words. He may be small, but he's strong in other ways.

I shake my head at his misunderstanding. "I mean, you have stamina and speed, a concoction that can make you stealthy."

His eyes light up. "Yeah?"

"Yeah. Have you ever done gymnastics?"

He rears back on his heels. "You think my dad would let me do gymnastics?"

I scrub a hand over my head and down my face. He's right. His dad never would allow him to. "Right. Well, that's where we'll start. Then we'll move on to other things." I let the latter linger in the air.

"How come?"

Throwing an arm over his shoulder, I tug him beneath me. "Because Matty, you're about to become one of my best secret weapons."

"How?"

"Because nobody will suspect you, so no one will ever see it coming." My grin becomes villainous as we head toward the gym while his eyes light up like the Fourth of July.

There's more to this kid than meets the eye.

So much more, and I'm about to help him discover it.

Chapter Forty-Four

Hallie

This week has been crazy. Rocco gave up school, and I miss him and his cocky smile, not to mention the additional attention I received from him.

Matt has been quiet and detached, and he's avoided me like the plague. Yet I feel him watching me despite his refusal to speak to me.

I've sent him multiple messages, and each goes unanswered. Rocco says I need to give him time, but he's my son and I'm missing out on what little time I had with him anyway.

Rocco has now moved in with me, and I can't say I'm mad about his insistence on being close to me whenever possible. The man is obsessed with my body, every inch of it, and I give it to him willingly multiple times a day. He doesn't let me lift a finger, insisting on covering my body with lotion after every shower, and when I asked him if it had the extra ingredient, he smirked, making my pussy clench with anticipation.

There's something gratifying about knowing I've been marked by my husband with his cum and his knife. His possession of me is intoxicating, and I never want it to end.

When he arrives home late at night and climbs into bed beside me, I long for his touch, ignoring what he will have been doing in order to receive the marks on his body or the blood beneath his fingernails.

I'm not naïve. I know his life is full of criminal activities that Gerrard has spent years fighting against, and while that eats away at me, I believe Rocco when he reassures me that the circles he runs in aren't of the same business as them.

They don't hurt innocent people.

And that's something that can't be said for Gerrard and his family.

The man has learned his behavior from somewhere, and something tells me the way his father has spent years looking me up and down like nothing more than dirt on his shoe proves where those behaviors have come from.

I stir the sauce on the stove, lost in my own world, and my phone vibrates. Matty's name flashes on the screen, and I answer it immediately, my heart racing with exhilaration to finally hear from him.

"Matt?" I blow out a deep sigh of relief.

"Mom?" The panic in his voice has my spine snapping straight. "Can you pick me up?" he rushes out while

DECEPTION

out of breath, and my heart skips a beat. "Dad took my car keys, and I want to leave."

"What?" I press my fingers to my forehead as I try to figure out what the hell is happening. All I know is my son needs me. "Of course." I know how volatile Gerrard can be, but he's never had an argument with Matty, not to my knowledge anyway. My pulse races with trepidation. "Are you okay?"

"Me and Dad fell out. He knows, Mom. He knows about you and Rocco." Anxiety clutches at my chest, and I suck in a sharp breath. "He hit me."

Disbelief laced in disappointment slips from him, and my heart seizes for my son while my body coils tight.

The bastard hit him.

Because of me.

"Are you okay?" Tears spring to my eyes as I switch off the stove.

"I'm okay. C-c-can you pick me up?"

I grab my car keys, not needing to be asked again, then stumble as I rush to slip my feet into my sneakers.

"He stormed out of the house. I don't know when he'll be back."

"Okay." I blow out as I try to gain control of my racing emotions. I head toward the door. "Call me if he gets home before I get there, Matty. I don't want a showdown with him." Sickness wells in my stomach at the thought.

"I will." I nod as I head out the door. "I'm sorry for what I said, Mom." My heart skips a beat at him feeling like he needs to apologize again. "I'm really sorry." He sniffles, and I want nothing more than to pull him into my arms and tell him everything will be okay.

I open the car door and slide inside. "It's okay, I know you were mad. You don't need to apologize again, Matty."

"I do. Besides, being mad doesn't make it okay to speak to you like I did. I was being a dick. I'm nothing like him, Mom," he says with conviction, and my chest swells with pride.

"I know that." I smile and swipe away the tears. "I'll be as quick as I can."

"Be careful. I'm just packing my bag."

"See you soon. Love you."

"Love you too, Mom."

Then I start the engine and call Rocco. I know this is going to go to shit, but Matty is my son, and he will always come first.

Rocco

I deliver another swift kick to the piece of shit who has been stealing our product. We're already on high alert with the FBI crawling up our asses, and we've moved all shipments to go through the O'Connell family's warehouse, having to forfeit a cut to them, but there are still dumb assess who think they can screw us over.

Then I lean over him and grab his hair, yanking his head back and forcing him to cry out. "I'm about to fucking slaughter you." I smile, causing the scumbag to piss himself and my smile to grow wider. Jesus, I love the thrill of their terror.

Taking my knife from my holster, I stand on his arm, ignoring the crunch of his bones beneath me. Then I slam the thick blade into his flesh, forcing him to scream as I carve his hand from his limp form, much like I've threatened before now.

The shrill sound of my phone blaring out causes my

shoulders to sag, but I swipe at the sweat gathered on my forehead and tug it from my jeans pocket.

Instantly, a smile plays on my face at Hallie's red hair splayed out on my pillowcase filling the screen. "Little Red," I answer with a smirk while my cock takes note of her heavy sigh.

"I know you're going to be mad." My eyebrows furrow. "But I'm going to be really quick," she blurts, and the hairs on the back of my neck stand to attention. "I need to head over to pick Matty up from his house."

My body coils taut. "No."

The sound of her car engine in the background has anger seething through me. "Did you hear me? No, Hallie."

"H-he needs me, Rocco." She sniffles, and I fucking hate not being there for her, but she needs to listen. She doesn't realize how dangerous that family is.

"Listen to me. I said no, Hallie."

Turning to face Silas, I place my hand over the speaker. "Finish him." I nod to the piece of shit at my feet, and Silas gives me a chin lift as I head toward the door and shove my blade back in my holster.

"Well, I'm going. Gerrard isn't there. I need to pick Matty up, Rocco." The despair in her voice has my blood running cold.

"What happened?"

"He hit Matty but left. I want to fetch him before he comes back."

"He what?" I bellow, my shoulders bunch tight as a

surge of protectiveness rushes through me. How dare he touch him?

She sniffles, and my shoulders drop at the sound. I shake my head. "I don't want you going there alone, Hal. Just wait for me, please."

"Gerrard isn't there right now. I'm going to grab Matty and meet you back at my house."

Anger burns my blood. She's so damn adamant. "He needs me, Rocco."

I grind my jaw as I throw my leg over my motorbike, knowing I'm losing this battle. "I can be there in less than twenty minutes, Hallie."

"I'm five minutes away." Her voice wobbles, and I fucking hate it. "I want to be in and out before Gerrard comes back. I don't want any more trouble."

My teeth ache as I struggle to compose my budding temper. "Hallie, listen to me. I don't want you going there without me. It isn't safe."

"No. You listen to me. Matty called me, and I'm going. If Gerrard comes back and you're with me, it's going to start a war neither of us is prepared for." Her sharp tone leaves no room for argument, and when she ends the call, I contemplate throwing my phone.

"Fuck!" I shout.

Then, with shaky fingers, I dial Rafael. Something tells me I will need some motherfucking backup.

Chapter Forty-Five

Hallie

My blood races as I place the car into park and glance around the driveway again. There's no sign of Gerrard or his car. So I throw open the car door, tuck my phone inside my jeans pocket, and head toward the house.

Then I knock on the door and push it open. "Matty?"

Silence fills the air, and a creeping sense of foreboding slivers up my spine. "Matty?" I say, louder this time, wondering if he's upstairs despite him knowing I was coming straight over. He was in so much of a rush to get out of here I was sure he would be waiting for me.

My hands shake as I slip inside the house and close the door behind me. The sound of it clicking shut has me jolting. Then I take a deep breath, and as I exhale, movement comes from the family living room.

"Matty?"

My feet travel toward the sound without thinking, and when I push open the door, a strangled cry escapes me.

Kneeling on the floor is my son with his hair being yanked in order to keep his head upright. His bloody face has my heart crumbling as my feet draw to a standstill.

Gerrard's sinister smile spreads across his face, and for the first time in my life I see a man I no longer recognize.

Sure, he has always been abusive toward me, but he's never shown Matty any contempt. He's never lifted a finger to him. Our son simply existed. He was never the target of Gerrard's controlling behavior. He was simply not on his father's radar, and in the past, I would have been thankful for that, but now, now I'm terrified. This man has a darkness in his eyes that he only ever allowed me to see, a combination of jealousy and possessiveness that's destructive. Not protective like Rocco's.

My breath catches in my throat when Matty attempts to speak, but the callous way Gerrard sneers toward our son heightens my terror. He's simply a means to an end for him, and something tells me I'm the end.

Has this always been his plan? For Matty to tie me to him.

His gleaming eyes slice toward me. "I knew you'd arrive for your precious Matty." The way disdain oozes from his words has my pulse skyrocketing.

"Gerrard, you're hurting him," I cry out, and he curls his lip.

"He always was a pussy."

DECEPTION

Matty flinches, and I can't help but feel pleased he's coherent enough to react despite the cruel taunts of his father.

"Tell me, Hallie. How does it feel to know everything you hold dear to you is about to be taken away? Like you took it from me!" He screams the latter, and I jump at the aggression in his tone.

Awareness trickles through my veins, and when a smug smile encompasses his face, a wave of sickness washes over me.

"Did you really think I'd allow that piece of shit to take my place? Did you think I'd allow him to touch what's mine and get away with it?" His chuckle is lacking humor. "Oh, Hallie." He tsks. "You never really knew me at all. It's time you all learned your place. Don't you agree, Matty?"

He yanks Matty's head up and down like a puppet as my body vibrates with dread.

Rocco's in danger, and there's no way I can warn him.

Rocco

I weave in and out of the traffic, my blood pumping with adrenaline coursing through my veins. Why the fuck couldn't she just listen to me?

My gut tells me something will go down, and the fact those I care most about in the world are on the line has my mind locked on my target. To get to them as soon as possible.

A searing pain hits my shoulder, and my hand jerks the handlebars of my bike, causing me to swerve. I quickly regain control as warmth gushes down my spine, making me realize I've been shot.

Motherfucker.

I dip down as low as possible on the bike and flit between larger vehicles in the hope for cover.

The sound of revved engines has me using the surrounding buildings' windows as mirrors, and I can make out two SUVs with blacked-out windows gaining on me. When one flashes blue and red lights, I know without a shadow of doubt they're the ones after me, and vehicles begin moving out of the way, leaving me open and exposed.

There's a reason I'm being chased and shot at by undercover police, and it has nothing to do with any crimes and everything to do with Gerrard fucking Davis using every resource he has. I know right then and there the son of a bitch is making a play for Hallie and Matt, but he's ensuring I'm out of the way first. I rev my bike, more determined than ever to reach them.

He will try to take them from me, but I'll do everything in my power to stop him.

Another bullet slices through the air, hitting the truck in front of me as I duck low.

The car on my left gains speed, and the prick in the passenger seat lowers his window farther, aiming his gun in my direction as the SUV swerves closer toward me.

I quickly draw my gun from behind my back and aim back at him. Bullets fire from mine and his, but we both hold steadfast. Neither of us hit our target, and I grit my teeth in annoyance.

My breath stills as they inch closer, and the lights from the other vehicle reflecting in the windows around me tell me I'm running out of luck. The prick moves his gun and aims toward my tire, and just as he releases a shot and I brace for impact, an SUV comes out of nowhere. Rafael's behind the steering wheel, and determination flashes on his face as he plows his SUV head-on into the vehicle. The sound of the crash ricochets through the city as I turn my handlebars and speed up, pushing

DECEPTION

away the fact that my brother could be injured by saving me.

The second car has no choice but to skid as I take the first corner I see. The sooner I get rid of these fuckers, the better, and I'm on a motorbike, so I use that to my advantage. Twisting the throttle to full capacity, I whizz down the center of the city street, ignoring the blaring of horns as I lose the fuckers who dared to try to take me down.

At the back of my mind, I begin to dissect Gerrard's plan.

Will he have people on his street waiting for me? Probably not. He wouldn't want to pull the police into his private life, especially because he hit Matt.

Are the police who tried to take me down part of a police crackdown? Again, probably not. They went about it all the wrong way, with too many witnesses. They clearly used the lights to their advantage, and everything else was something Gerrard set up. I doubt if they're actually part of the FBI, probably his or his father's goons.

I slow down as I enter residential streets. The last thing I want is to draw any more attention to myself, or worse, hurt an innocent bystander.

When Gerrard's house comes into view and I see Hallie's car still parked there, my heart sinks. She should have left by now.

I know whatever I'm about to walk into is bad, and it sends my stomach plummeting.

Chapter Forty-Six

Rocco

I push open the front door and slip inside. The sound of Hallie crying has my heart free-falling, but I try to curb my temper and my uncontrollable need to comfort her, and use the time to try to figure out a plan.

Gerrard won't want police intervention; he won't want his work colleagues to know what a scumbag he actually is. The high society people him and his family claim him to be is a mask they wear. Whereas, I wear none.

I hide behind nothing.

I'm the Mafia and proud of it.

My fingers shake as I type out a message to Silas.

> Me: Call 911 domestic disturbance to Gerrard's.

> Silas: You need backup?

I contemplate his question and decide not to take him up on his offer. The more people I pull into this, the more shit I bring down on the family, and that's going to make it harder for us to get out of this mess.

My shoulder pinches with the gunshot wound as I type a response.

> Me: I'm good. Have doc on standby at dad's.

> Silas: Try not to die.

I smirk. It's as good as wishing me luck, and something tells me I will need it.

Inching closer to the room, I keep my back against the wall.

"You married the little cunt? Hm, that's the sort of whore you are. You married him to spite me!"

Every muscle in my body stiffens as I listen in on his tirade.

"I-It's not like that." Hallie sobs. "You're hurting him. Just let him go." Her words have my vision blurring. He's hurting Matt. Every instinct in my body comes alive to protect my family, and I'm done being slick. I push away from the wall and let him know I'm here.

"It's me you want, you piece of shit," I grit out as I step into the open doorway, and my eyes land on Matt. My nostrils flare at my best friend's bloody face. His eyes roll, and my knuckles ache from how hard I'm pumping my fists.

He touched what's mine.

He hurt what's mine.

They're mine to protect.

His dark chuckle fills the room, and with each rise of his chest, I imagine slicing through him with my knife. Causing him the same pain as he caused them, only worse. I'll leave him bare of his skin for touching what doesn't belong to him.

"Here he is. The boy. The criminal," he mocks, then withdraws a gun from behind his back. Hallie stumbles backward, her back flush against the wall beside them. My skin crawls to get to her, but I'm cautious of any sudden movement that could encourage him to lash out.

"Did you know this manipulative piece of shit owns that house you live in?"

Hallie flinches on his words, and I kick myself for not explaining everything sooner. His grin is full of jest, and I want to throat punch him for it. "Owns the whole goddamn street, isn't that right?" I feel her eyes on mine but don't dare look, not when he's so unpredictable.

"You know he set me up too, right? It was him that fucking drugged me! I never slept with no goddamn woman! He drugged me so you'd divorce me! He fucking set me up!" He gets louder and louder with each word, and I can feel the heat of Hallie's stare on the side of my face.

"Is that true?" she whispers brokenly. "Rocco? You deceived me? You lied to me." It isn't a question, a statement. A fact. I deceived her. And I'd do it all again to have her.

I flick my eyes over to her. "I did." The hurt swims in her eyes, and I hate myself for putting it there.

"He made friends with Matt to get close to you both."

Matt's bloodshot eyes meet mine, and I swallow back the truth and guilt from his words.

"He set this all up." Gerrard sweeps his arm out, then tugs on his hair. "He stole you from me, and now I'm taking you back."

The manipulation I've forced them to endure hangs in the air, but I try to remain on target, to get them to safety. I clear my throat and hold my hands out in front of me so he can see I'm not a threat. "You don't want to hurt them, Gerrard. It's me you want. Just let them go."

"They're my fucking family, not yours. I won't ever let them go," he spits out through gritted teeth, and his words penetrate my soul. He means every damn word he says; he won't let them go. He never had any intentions of ever letting them go, and my stomach clenches at the notion.

"Then let them leave the room. They don't need to be drawn into this anymore than they are already."

Hallie's eyes dart from mine to Gerrard's.

"Hallie can patch Matty up."

"Matty?" He tilts his head as if examining me, and I wince at my slip up. I've exposed how much Matt means to me. Gerrard's eyes narrow on Hallie, and my spine bolts straight while I sidestep toward her, inching closer

DECEPTION

in the hope that if I stand between us, I can give her a fighting chance to get out of here unscathed.

He turns his attention back to me, and I still my movements. "What do you fucking care about my son? You don't think I know you knocked up my wife?"

It's on the tip of my tongue to correct him that she's my wife, but I refrain from angering him further.

"Maybe I should take your kid from you like you're taking mine from me?" He raises the gun toward Hallie, and my breath stills. As if in slow motion, Matty finds an inner strength only I knew him to have before now. He slips from Gerrard's hand and drops to the floor, then tucks his shoulder under just how I taught him and delivers a slick forward roll with a high kick to Gerrard's hand that knocks him off balance. Then he rises between him and his mom. My breath stutters as his battered body hobbles to stand in front of his mom, and I couldn't be prouder.

"I won't let you hurt them." His shaky words pierce my hard shell, warming my bones while simultaneously shattering them. My best friend is putting himself in the firing line for my girl, my baby too.

Gerrard steps back, and his laugh makes the hairs on the back of my neck stand on end, and as if in slow motion, he raises the gun. "I can hurt her another way." He presses the trigger. "Son," he spits out, as if he's an afterthought.

My best friend.

My wife's baby, her son.

My stepson.

And he will hurt him as if he's nothing.

My heart ceases to beat as Hallie's pained cry rings out in my ears, and I lunge in front of him as two bullets leave the gun. The shots play out like background noise, and all I can think is I hope I saved him as my world tilts on an axis and becomes black.

I hope I saved him, for her.

Hallie

His wild eyes tell me everything I need to know. He's out for vengeance, for blood, and he doesn't care who he hurts to get it, and ultimately, he wants to hurt me.

Matty stands in front of me, and my legs almost give way as my hand rests on the small bump beneath my summer dress.

He raises his gun, and I see everything in slow motion.

Gerrard never cared about Matty. He was simply a reason to keep me, and when he realizes he can't, he turns his attention toward Matty to hurt me the most.

He holds the gun in front of my son, and when his finger presses down on the trigger, my legs almost give out.

Rocco moves so fast I don't see him coming. He launches himself in the air as terror grips my heart in a vise, and two shots fill my ears and force my heart to still.

One.

Two.

Then Rocco falls to the floor with a heavy thud, taking a part of me with him.

This man.

My husband. My son's best friend. Took bullets to protect Matty. He did what he promised, to always put me and my son first, our family.

Matty falls to the floor beside him and cradles Rocco's face in his hands while I remain standing somehow. Lost between my hatred for the man before me and my heart breaking at the scene I'm witnessing, too despondent to react.

"You son of a bitch!" Matty screams as he lifts his head to face his father. The fury in my usual gentle son is unheard of.

Gerrard lifts the gun once again, but Matty moves quicker and slips a knife from beneath Rocco's jacket and throws it in Gerrard's direction.

His aim shocks me, as if he knows what he's doing. But he couldn't, could he?

The knife lodges in Gerrard's chest, then his mouth falls open and his eyes widen as he makes a gurgle before he slowly falls to his knees.

My instincts finally kick in, and I scramble past Matty and Rocco to knock the gun from his hands, kicking it across the room as sounds of the emergency services descend on the street.

"Mom! Help him."

The anguish in Matty's voice has my head snapping in his direction. "Please help him." Tears flow down his

DECEPTION

face as he rocks Rocco in his arms. "I'm sorry. I'm so fucking sorry, Rocco. I'll be the best big brother, I promise. I fucking promise."

Blood pools around Rocco's chest, and I rush toward him. "Your shirt. Give me your shirt."

Matty tugs his T-shirt over his head and presses it to Rocco's chest. "Hold it there, Matty." Tears stream down my face while footsteps approach. "We love you. We love you so much. Promise me you won't leave us," I whisper as an emergency responder rushes through the door and takes over.

"Promise me you won't leave. Our little girl needs you. She needs you and we do too," I state as those sweet, traitorous lips of his turn blue, and I want nothing more than to kiss the life back into them, uncaring of how we got here. Truthfully, none of it matters anymore. The only thing that matters is that there's an us.

Chapter Forty-Seven

Hallie

Four months later ...

I spent six weeks at Rocco's hospital bedside, where he was recovering from three bullet wounds. One in his shoulder, and two in his chest. The man insists he's invincible and says he's stronger than ever with Matty at his side. I don't know whether to feel relief at his comment or concern.

After the police swarmed the house, Matty was arrested. He insisted I go with Rocco to the hospital, and I was torn between being by his side or my husband's. Thankfully, Rafael offered to step in to be there for Matty as he was charged with second-degree murder. The Marino family has an incredible legal team who got the case thrown out after they discovered Gerrard's use of illegal police resources.

In order for my ex-father-in-law to keep his job and his reputation, he threw his son under the bus and made sure to let law enforcement know that he had no knowledge of his Gerrard's misdeeds. Of course he was portrayed as an upstanding citizen, disgusted with his son's actions. We both know that's untrue, and at the risk of feeling his wrath, I kept my mouth shut when some topics came to light that I don't believe my ex was a part of.

However, Rocco reassures me that Harrison Davis will get what's coming to him too, and I believe every word of it.

When Rocco was discharged from the hospital, Matty drove us home, back to my little house with the white picket fence that I came to discover belonged to Rocco.

As soon as we sat down and talked about what really brought us together, I was stunned, but in a twisted way, I was thankful too. Rocco provided a sense of security I have never felt before, an overwhelming happiness and highs of pleasure I never knew existed.

Until him.

He's dangerous, deceitful, and depraved, but he's mine.

"Have you been waiting up for me, Little Red?"

"Yes, Daddy." I bite into my lip.

He kicks off his combat boots and socks, then throws his leather jacket onto the chair in the corner of the room and lifts his T-shirt over his head, exposing his ripped abs and the deep V with a soft trail of hair that falls below the waistband of his jeans.

Then he crawls onto the edge of the bed. "Does my little red want licked?"

My core clenches with his filthy words as he holds my gaze, and I push back the hair that's fallen in his eyes. He snags my wrist before bringing my hand to his mouth and placing soft kisses over my fingers, then he sucks two fingers into his mouth before abruptly dropping them.

"Play with your cunt, Little Red, Daddy's going to fill your ass." My cheeks heat as I use my fingers to separate my already slick folds. Then my husband drops his jeans, and his rock-hard cock bounces off his washboard abs, and my mouth waters to savor the pre-cum sticking to him.

Jesus, he's hot, and he's all mine. Every delicious inch of him.

Rocco

My cock drips with vigor, desperate to enter her pregnant body. "You're so fucking beautiful, Little Red." I sigh as I fist my aching solid length.

"Thank you, Daddy." Her cheeks still heat on my moniker, but I love it.

"I want you to spit on my cock, Little Red. Get Daddy's cock nice and wet for your little hole so he doesn't make you bleed." Her chest rises as I crawl toward her mouth. Her hot breath warms my cock, and I close my eyes when she leans forward, delivering her spittle onto the tip like the good girl she is. My fingers tangle in her hair as I stroke over her head with praise. "Again, baby, get Daddy nice and wet with your spit."

The moment her wetness hits the head of my cock, I use it to lube it up, pumping my fist up and down my steel girth, then I move between her legs and push open her thighs. Her huge bump sits between us while she leans up on her elbows to watch me take her. At thirty-seven weeks pregnant, she's the most stunning I've ever seen her, and I want her pregnancy to last forever. "Play with your clit like a good girl."

She moves her fingers on command, and I feel like a warrior, wielding control and exuding power. Then I take the head of my cock and slide it up and down her slick, wet pussy, delighting in the way she arches into me as I do. Then I place the tip at her puckered hole.

Gently, I push inside. "Let me in, Little Red. Let Daddy inside to play with you." Her fingers work faster as I push in deeper. "Daddy wants to paint you with his pleasure."

"Oh fuck," she mewls as I slide farther inside. My muscles are coiled tight as I try my best to combat the need to fuck her aggressively. I want to savor every whimper, every mewl of pleasure that her little lips pout.

When one hand moves to squeeze her tit roughly, all bets are off. Breast play is my kink, and the moment I discovered I could stimulate milk from her nipple before baby red is born, it became my new pastime. I slam inside her like a feral animal and lean over our bump to grab her tit and suck the peaked bud roughly into my mouth.

I groan as the first drop of milk falls onto my tongue, causing my eyes to roll in ecstasy. Jesus, I can't wait until she can cover me in her milk.

Her fingers clutch the back of my head, holding me in place, and her fingernails dig into my scalp. The fact she loves this as much as me makes my hips move quicker, filling her tight ass with my thick cock. Each stretch of

DECEPTION

her muscles as I enter her has my balls drawing up with insatiable need.

"Fuck, mama, you taste so damn good."

"Yes." Her fingers work quicker between us as I try my best not to squish our baby. "Yes. Daddy!" Her body tightens, and her heavy pants turn to sounds of pleasure as my cock finally relents, and with one final slam, I fill her hole with ropes upon ropes of my thick hot cum.

"Fuck," I garble, then suck harder on her nipple to draw out the pleasure.

When my orgasm eases, my suckle turns gentler and so does her caress of my scalp, and I mewl in contentment.

Then I roll us to our sides as my cock slips from her ass. A deluge of cum falls between us, and I hate it not being used.

"Oh shit!" A strangled, pained sound leaves Hallie's throat.

I dart up. "What's wrong?"

"I think my water just broke."

My eyes widen as panic rushes through me at an alarming pace.

I've dealt with murderers, drug lords, and traffickers, and I've slaughtered, maimed, and tortured, but never have I come close to this feeling of nervousness.

I scrub a hand through my hair as my eyes dart around the room.

Are we ready?

Am I good enough to be a father?

Do I have everything we need?

Am I everything she needs?

Her soft hand slides down my spine, causing me to shudder, then I turn to face her, and her controlled smile sends a feeling of relief through my coiled muscles. "You're ready," she says with a nod.

My lip twitches when I realize I voiced my concerns, but seeing her confidence in me has my chest puffing with pride.

"Damn fucking right I'm ready, Little Red. Let's do this!"

I wasn't ready.

How can any fucker be ready to watch a room of strangers descend on their girl? Touching your girl.

Seeing her naked and bare.

How can any man be ready when their girl's legs are open wide while countless eyes settle on her pussy?

And how the fuck can you be ready when that pussy expands so fucking big you can almost fit your head in it while your girl roars in pain, and you know you caused all of it?

And when they place your baby in your arms, how can any man prepare for that?

This tiny weight, now completely dependent on you and your ability to step up. How can you truly be ready for it?

I'm not sure, but I sure as hell will do my best to try.

Chapter Forty-Eight

Rocco

I stare down at our daughter—Seraphina, Phi for short—on my chest, and my heart swells. She's the most beautiful little thing I've ever seen. Her name means "fiery one," and I intend on her being just that. Even at four weeks old, I can see the red in her hair, and I know she will be a mini-Hallie, and I love the idea.

Matt has been an amazing big brother and best friend, and he reminds me daily that he's not calling me daddy. I smile to myself while fighting the urge to tell him I'm his mom's daddy, and she loves calling me it. Something tells me it wouldn't go down well and what bridges we've built would probably be obliterated.

Matt moved in with us at our house and has been working his ass off at the gym. The kid has some incredible moves, and if it wasn't for Hallie begging me not to, I'd have signed him up for MMA fighting. But what she doesn't know won't hurt her. If I point him in the direction of the underground clubs, it's not my fault if he walks through the doors, signs up, and kicks ass.

"You know she isn't going to settle in her crib if you keep letting her sleep on your chest." Her soft voice caresses me, and I glance up to find her epic curves tucked into sleep shorts and a camisole top that emphasizes her amazing rack.

"I was just waiting for you to finish up marking your assignments." Ever since the incident with Gerrard, Hallie has taken time off from school and teaches online courses, mainly because she wants to be home with Phi, and who am I to argue? The last thing I want is some dumbass student eyeing up my girl and her huge tits.

The thought of her tits has my cock stirring, and I lick my lips. Yeah, time to move. The last thing I want around my daughter is a hard cock.

I slide off the bed and head toward the nursery. "Come on, little firecracker, let Papa put you to bed."

"And don't be long!" she shouts as I head through the door. There's not a chance in hell I'm being drawn in to watch her cute sleepy form.

"Not tonight," I whisper as I place her down in her crib.

Not when Daddy needs to be fed.

Hallie

Watching Rocco with Phi has my core clenching. There's something erotic about a man with a bare chest and a tiny baby sleeping on him while his large palm strokes over the baby's back and cute little tush.

Rocco is everything I want as a father to my children, and that has only emphasized Gerrard's lack of parenting skills.

The bond between him and Matt has become brotherly, but with Phi, it's all about being her papa. I insisted on us not encouraging daddy, as that's too close to what we have. It's personal and intimate, it's everything. He's my protector, my giver, and I'm simply his.

I slide my shorts down and lift the camisole over my head, then climb onto the mattress with my back against the pillows and open my legs and wait.

The last time I did this, he took longer putting Phi down than expected and I had two orgasms before he joined me. This time, I'm hoping he can deliver them.

All of them.

My head snaps up to find him in the doorway, his chiseled body looking as edible as ever.

How is it men can look incredibly hot as new parents, but women get all the hang-ups—the stretch marks and leaky boobs.

Something I would be conscious of if it wasn't for Rocco having me feeling like the only woman in the world he has eyes for. His loyalty has never once been in doubt. I feel adored by the man I love, and the feeling is mutual.

My gaze roams over him as pushes his boxers to the floor, then he stalks toward me like a predator hunting his prey. "Spread those pussy lips for me, Little Red. Let Daddy see you nice and open for him. I like to see where I'm sliding my cock."

He climbs onto the bed toward me until his face is between my legs, watching me open myself up to him, then his eyes connect with mine, and he delivers a long stream of spittle onto my fingers, our eyes never disconnecting.

My fingers become wetter, a combination of his spit and my arousal. I fidget as pleasure zips up my spine, and he slides his finger through the mixture and brings it to my clit. Tilting my head back, he strokes me with slow circles, and I lift my hips in encouragement.

"Does my baby need attention?"

"Yes," I pant out wantonly.

"Do you need Daddy to help you?" He licks his lips.

DECEPTION

"Yes, please."

My body sags as he removes his hand and uses both hands to push my tits together. There's still milk in them since Phi doesn't drink it all, but her papa won't let it go to waste.

He moves forward and pushes my tits together; they're engorged and achy, and the moment his lips locks around my nipples, I moan. The vibration of his growl as my milk splashes into his mouth has me on the edge, and I lean forward to adjust his cock, loving the way he flinches when I touch him.

"Fuck," he hisses as I position the tip at my center, then he pushes inside, causing my eyes to roll at the sensation of feeling so full.

His hips withdraw and he snaps them forward just as quick, and the headboard bangs against the wall.

He detaches his lips, and his nostrils flare. With one hand, he grips the headboard above me. "Fuck, you taste so damn good." Milk drips from his mouth and down his chin as he stares down at my leaking tits bouncing as he fucks me faster and faster. Harder and harder. He wraps his other palm around my throat, and I thrust up into him. "That's it. Take Daddy's thick cock in your pussy. Leak your milk, Little Red. Daddy will lick you clean."

His cock rubs inside me so perfectly, so well-practiced that my orgasm slams into me, and his hand tightens as his own becomes evident. "Fuck yeah, just like that, Little Red. Milk Daddy's cock." *Slam.* "Just." *Thrust.* "Like." *Slam.* "That."

His cum hits my walls, and we spiral into a realm of pleasure created just for us.

My vision becomes blurry as he whispers, "Daddy's little red."

Epilogue

Rocco

Two months later ...

My gaze never wavers from Hallie's, and her cheeks flame as if feeling the heat of my stare on her. When she turns her head, I tilt mine toward my father's office, and her blush deepens as she shakes her head.

"That sly fucker, Robert, is here again. What the fuck is he doing here?" Rafael seethes from beside me, and I give him a shrug, uncaring that our once-upon-a-time stepbrother is at our father's mansion despite taking guilt money from our father but not showing his face at invited dinners for years now. Although, he has been scoping out the Halloween party for two years in a row.

Adrenaline zips up my spine as I stare at my wife,

and I press the small control I have in my pocket again, and her body becomes rigid, then I release it and nod toward my father's office again.

When I placed the little clit stimulator in her G-string, she scrunched her nose up at it, but I've spent all evening tormenting her with the little device.

I can feel the heat of Rafael's stare on my face, and anger surges through me when he glances toward Hallie, then our father's office, clearly not missing my intentions. "Jesus. I don't know what you plan on doing, but it's not a good idea," he hisses into my ear.

My lip quirks as he pulls back. "Funny you have an opinion on how I choose to fuck my wife. Pretty sure last year you went all primal and fucked Ellie's ass while she wore her school uniform in the forest." I tilt my head toward the forest just beyond the patio.

Rafael shifts from side to side. "How?"

I scoff. "Poor fucking girl could barely walk. I drove her home too, remember?"

He makes a noncommittal sound in the back of his throat. "Your fucking funeral," he grunts, then walks away, leaving me to assess my beautiful deception.

The schoolteacher outfit she's wearing to our family's annual Halloween party is extreme, and my cock approves. She finally makes an excuse to leave the conversation with some woman dressed as a cat, then turns on her high heels.

Full hips sway as she makes her way toward the open office door. The pencil skirt she wears is covering the garters I chose for her. Her hair is in a loose bun at the

DECEPTION

base of her neck, and her white blouse is stretched tightly over her epic tits. To finish the look, she wears glasses, looking a combination between a schoolteacher and a secretary. My mind goes to the former as my cock throbs increasingly hard against my jeans.

I stride toward her, ignoring the subtle glances my way as I do

Then when she enters the room, I follow inside and close the door, flicking the lock in the process.

The room is laced in darkness, with only a sliver of light coming from under the door.

I could flip the switch, but what fun would that be?

"Little Red?"

Her perfume infiltrates my nostrils, and I pop open my jean button to save time for the inevitable. Her breathing picks up when she hears my zipper, and my eyes narrow in on the couch.

"Has my teacher been a naughty girl today?"

"No," she says, giving away her location.

"Men have been looking at what's mine, Little Red." I walk toward her.

"I'm sorry, Daddy," she whispers, but sounds anything but sorry.

"Hm." I take a hold of her ankle and flip her, then drag her over the arm of the couch and push her skirt up to give me the best view of her perfect round ass. The sweet sound of her startled gasp has me pulling my cock from my jeans to relieve it. My fingers rub over the tip, and I have to squeeze it to curb my desperation.

"You dress like this for me?" I can make the outline of

her G-string out, the one I chose for her to wear for this little role play. Then I pull my hand back and slap her ass sharply. A heavy pant fills the room when I deliver her with another. "Fucking answer me!"

"Yes, Daddy."

"Such a dirty, slutty teacher, Little Red."

I deliver another swift smack, and my cock jumps to life to get in on the action. "A filthy fucking teacher that likes her student to fill her up."

"Yes." She squeals when I slap her ass cheek again.

Deftly, I shrug off my leather jacket, letting it pool to the floor, then I remove my knife and glide it over her ass. Knowing she wears my mark has my blood pumping with a wild need to claim her, to put another baby in her belly. Another little red. Like her mama.

"Please, Daddy." She begs so beautifully, so I lean over her and spit on her ass, and she shudders at the impact.

Then I use my knife to slice through the flimsy fabric of her panties.

"They're so wet, Little Red."

"Mmm."

I kick her legs farther apart, then grab her hair and yank it from the bun, delighting when her mass of red waves brushes my fingers.

"Open your mouth, teacher."

She does as I ask, and I stuff the fabric in my hand into her mouth. Her heavy breaths fill the room as I slide the head of my cock up and down her dripping pussy, and I almost combust at the sounds lodging in her throat.

DECEPTION

Then I flip the knife so the blade is in my palm and use the handle to press on her asshole. A garbled noise leaves her as I push my knife handle and cock head into her at the same time.

"I'm going to fuck my baby into my teacher."

She isn't on birth control, not yet, despite her questioning if she should. But I insisted she shouldn't.

My hips move in time with the knife, pump after pump as pain lances through my palm, the pressure causing it to cut me deep. Sounds of our skin slapping together fill the air.

"You have some milk in those big tits for Daddy?"

A noise leaves her throat, and I laugh as I slam inside her deeper. Her body rubs against the arm of the chair, and the friction I cause must be working because her body tightens beneath me, pulling the cum from my balls as I bottom out and lodge myself as deep as possible.

"That's it. Take all that cum and breed for Daddy." A muffled scream fills the air, and my mouth falls slack at the impact of my orgasm as I cum deep inside my wife.

The handle to the door moves, and I still. Our heavy breaths mingle with the panic rippling up my spine.

There's only one person this could be. My father.

And if he finds me fucking Hallie in here, I'm pretty damn sure I will be missing a ball, especially with the fallout of the Harrington family lingering.

I pull out of Hallie and quickly zip up my jeans while she scrambles to pull down her skirt. Blood drips from my hand, and I swipe it on my T-shirt while tucking my knife safely in its holster. Then I grab my jacket and shrug it on.

She shoves her ripped panties into my pocket as the lock disengages. Her wide eyes meet mine, and I pull her toward the heavy drapes that cover my father's balcony.

The door opens and the lights come on, but we're blanketed in darkness, and I can't help but slide the tips of my fingers into Hallie's slick pussy. She glares at me, and I bite into my lip to stop from chuckling.

"In here, Little Pet." My father's deep voice fills the room, and I squeeze my eyes closed as I imagine him bringing in another submissive, not something I want my wife to witness. Even if she can't see it, she will be able to hear it.

All of it. I grimace at the thought.

"Why do you call me that?" a small voice whispers, and the innocence behind it turns my stomach. She's young. Not something I'm into, but it seems my father doesn't have the same preferences. At least he's not like those scumbags who don't even wait for girls to come of age; my father has always been firm on that belief. Still, the thoughts of my father in his fifties and a young girl is repulsive. I repress a shudder bursting to get out.

"Because you're my pet. Tell me, Little Pet, do you normally go into rooms with men you don't know?"

The guy is good, I'll give him that. His smooth voice is reserved purely for the women he beds.

"I-I don't." Jesus, the poor girl will be eaten alive, but I guess she'll die happy. I smile to myself at the thought while Hallie continues to drill holes in my head with her death glare.

"Are you going to let Daddy play with you?"

Oh, sweet Jesus. I pinch the bridge of my nose and close my eyes.

"What sort of play?"

I repress a choke as Hallie's mouth falls open.

"Daddy wants to gag these little lips with his leather belt." Oh, hell no. Think Rocco, think. "Put a collar on this soft delicate neck of yours, and he's going to splash his cum all over this pretty little face, then I'm going to flip you over and use all your tiny holes while you scream out your pleasure."

"C-collar me?"

"Hm, a leash too."

"A leash?" The poor girl sounds like she's about to bolt for the door.

"Then Daddy is going to take good care of you. What do you say, Little Pet?"

"Y-yes," she breathes out hesitantly, shocking the shit out of me, and Hallie's puzzled gaze reaches mine.

"Come, let me take you somewhere special."

I bite into my fisted knuckles to stop myself from laughing. My father's idea of special is a specifically adapted sex dungeon in one of his many clubs.

"Okay," she murmurs.

I hold my breath as the footsteps move toward the door, then the handle turns, and relief floods me.

I wait for the door to click shut, but it doesn't, making my eyebrows furrow in confusion. "Rocco?" My father's stern voice fills the room, causing Hallie to startle beside me as her fingers curl in my hand.

"Get this fucking office fumigated, you little shit."

"Yes, sir." I grin.

"Guess his hearing isn't so bad, after all." I wink at my wife.

THE END

Are you ready for Daddy Vinny's book?

Coming in 2025, preorder it here: DOMINATION

MORE?

Did you know **DECEPTION** is part of the Mafia Daddies Series?
Here is the reading order:
Book 1 Daddy's Addiction
Book 2 POSSESSION
Book 3 DECEPTION
Book 4 DOMINATION

Would you like a sneak peek of Daddy Tommy from Daddy's Addiction?
You can grab it here: Daddy's Addiction Scene

Acknowledgments

Tee the lady that started it all for me. Thank you for an eternity.

I must start with where it all began, TL Swan. When I started reading your books, I never realized I was in a place I needed pulling out of. Your stories brought me back to myself.

With your constant support and the network created as 'Cygnet Inkers' I was able to create something I never realized was possible, I genuinely thought I'd had my day. You made me realize tomorrow is just the beginning.

SPECIAL MENTION

Kate, thank you for loving Rocco as much as me.

Jaclyn, thank you for all your support and advice.

Lilibet, you're amazing and I appreciate you.

Jo, I feel so privileged to have you onboard. Thank you!

My Incredible ARC and Street Teams.

To all of you, I appreciate you all more than you know!

My Reckless Readers!

THANK YOU! Your support means so much to me. Thank you for gifting me with your time, photos, games and laughs.

To my world.

Boys, what are you doing reading this?

To my hubby, the J in my BJ.

Our dreams are becoming a reality and I couldn't have achieved them without you. Thank you for believing in me.

Without you I wouldn't be BJ Alpha. Love you trillions!

And finally…

Thank you to you, my readers. I really couldn't do this without you.
Love Always
BJ Alpha. X

About the Author

BJ Alpha lives in the UK with her hubby, two teenage sons and three fur babies.
She loves to write and read about hot, alpha males and feisty females.

Follow me on my social media pages:
Facebook: BJ Alpha
My Facebook readers group: BJ Alpha's Reckless Readers
Instagram: BJ Alpha

Also by BJ ALPHA

MAFIA DADDIES
Daddy's Addiction
POSSESSION
DECEPTION
DOMINATION

SECRETS AND LIES SERIES
CAL Book 1
CON Book 2
FINN Book 3
BREN Book 4
OSCAR Book 5
THE FINAL VOW
O'CONNELL'S FOREVER

BORN SERIES
BORN RECKLESS

THE BRUTAL DUET
HIDDEN IN BRUTAL DEVOTION
LOVE IN BRUTAL DEVOTION

THE BRUTAL DUET PART TWO
BRUTAL SECRETS

BRUTAL LIES

STORM ENTERPRISES
SHAW Book 1

TATE Book 2

OWEN Book 3

VEILED IN SERIES
VEILED IN HATE

CARRERA FAMILY
STONE

(A Secrets and Lies Crossover)

Printed in Dunstable, United Kingdom